"A many-layered book. Ouida Sebestyen has wrapped story in poetry, wrapped me with it, too, caught me and held me, made me feel."

—Cynthia King,
The New York Times

"Sebestyen plays no holds barred the first chapter and doesn't let up . . . audiences must meet this story head–on . . . the book is a finely honed heart-wrencher."

—*School Library Journal*

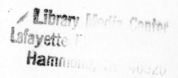
discrimination . . . ... black family strong in their love and pride."

—*Bulletin of the Center for Children's Books*

WORDS
BY HEART

Ouida Sebestyen

BANTAM BOOKS
TORONTO • NEW YORK • LONDON • SYDNEY • AUCKLAND

This low-priced Bantam Book
has been completely reset in a typeface
designed for easy reading, and was printed
from new plates. It contains the complete
text of the original hard-cover edition.
NOT ONE WORD HAS BEEN OMITTED.

RL 5, IL age 10 and up

WORDS BY HEART

A Bantam Book / published by arrangement with
Little, Brown and Company

PRINTING HISTORY

Little Brown edition published June 1979
2 printings through April 1980

A Selection of Reader's Digest Condensed Books August 1979

The first two chapters of this novel are based in part on the
author's short story, "Words by Heart," originally published in
December 1968 by Ingenue.

Bantam edition / July 1981
2nd printing . . . November 1983
3rd printing . . . January 1986

Starfire and accompanying logo of a stylized star are
registered trademarks of Bantam Books, Inc.
Registered in U.S. Patent and Trademark Office and elsewhere.

ISBN 0-553-25900-8

Published simultaneously in the United States and Canada

Bantam Books are published by Bantam Books, Inc. Its trademark,
consisting of the words "Bantam Books" and the portrayal of a rooster, is
Registered in U.S. Patent and Trademark Office and in other countries.
Marca Registrada. Bantam Books, Inc., 666 Fifth Avenue, New York,
New York 10103.

PRINTED IN THE UNITED STATES OF AMERICA

O   12   11   10

To Gran'ma

One

OLD BULLET HAD GUESSED they were going somewhere—Lena's folks—before they came out the door.
He stood under the wagon like a spare horse, wagging
hopefully. Ben Sills's family hadn't mingled much since
they came from Scattercreek, where everyone was black,
to this town where no one was. But tonight was a special
night, Lena's night, when her Magic Mind was going
to matter, not her skin.

As they were leaving, a firefly star winked out over
the roof of the rent-house they had lived in that summer.
Lena asked up at it, Is tonight when my whole life
changes? Wishing on it for the thing she wanted would
have been admitting she doubted herself. So she only
asked.

Her papa and step-mama rode on the wagon seat.
Lena sat in the back with the little kids, jouncing like
a meal sack while her stiff-starched dress mashed to
smithers. Bethel Springs Schoolhouse, where they were
going for the contest, was used for grade school on
weekdays and for church on Sundays, now that the

1

dance hall was gone. Before that, folks had gone to church in the big solid-floored Melodyland with a real piano up front. But the congregation prayed mightily every Sunday that this blight on the community would be banished, and one afternoon during an electrical storm, it was. Of course, they didn't have a church either after that, and had to use the schoolhouse. Papa said God taught us a lesson sometimes by giving us what we asked for.

Bullet followed them a way and stopped in the ruts, making sad sweeps with his tail.

When they turned out into the main road they had to ease around two of the redheaded Haney boys sitting double on their daddy's cutting horse. They were planted firmly in the middle of the road like the statue of a two-headed general. The little head belonged to Sammy, the one the kids laughed at in school because he brought a turnip for his lunch. He peeped out at them from behind his nearly grown brother Tater, but Tater stared out over their heads, ignoring Papa's nod even though his daddy worked for Mrs. Chism the same as Papa did. As he dwindled away he held his marble pose.

Lena's step-mama, Claudie, murmured, "Still smarting."

Papa nodded. Tater's daddy had got fired from the gin for drinking, and Papa had taken his place.

As they creaked down the road, the few folks who passed them looked back in mild curiosity. Lena gazed straight ahead the way Tater Haney had, wondering if they could see on her face what this night meant.

When they got to the schoolhouse, the yard was already full of wagons and buggies. Lena jumped down heavily and smoothed her dress with hands that were damp in the cool October dusk. She hoisted Roy and Armilla down, and swung the baby into Claudie's arms. They were late. She would die the way she always did when she walked in on the loud boards and all those faces, like an orchard of pink-cheeked peaches, turned toward her. But they couldn't have kept her away that night, not with a log chain. She was pushing the little kids toward the door when she felt her step-mama's hand drop onto her shoulder. She spun around in surprise.

"Lena," Claudie said quickly, having put off what she meant to say until it was almost too late, "Lena, this kind of game—can't everybody win. So you mustn't take it hard if you don't. Second place, or third place—"

Lena pulled away as though the hand had scorched her. I'm going to win, she said inside. It's not a game and I'm going to *win*. But she couldn't say that to Claudie—she couldn't say, I'm going to show you and Papa, and Winslow Starnes, and everybody! Because deep in her heart she wasn't sure she could win, in spite of all her praying.

They went in. The preacher was talking. He nodded his clean bald head to greet them and went on saying, ". . . good wholesome fun, while at the same time it serves to turn the thoughts of our young people toward the blessed words of the Scriptures. So I will turn the program over to Mr. Jaybird Kelsey, who had the idea for this contest and worked it out."

He sat down beside the map of Friday's geography lesson, and Jaybird Kelsey got up and sidled to the teacher's desk on the little platform. Jaybird Kelsey was a good man, everybody said, a deacon and a cornerstone and all that, but he had some uppity ideas sometimes, like the frizzled chin whiskers he wore that were meant to give him dignity, but really made him look like a goat.

"All right, boys and girls," he said, "let's all come up here and stand in a row." He gave his stomach a pat, like a make-believe Santa Claus. "I've got a prize for the winner, now, so you all do your best. You just have to quote the verse of Scripture, you don't have to give the book it's from. But you do have to recite a verse when it's your time, or you drop out. Understand?"

They straggled to the front of the room, grinning and elbowing as they formed a line. Lena's heart began to thud as she walked forward in Claudie's neat, buttoned shoes with the clacking heels. There were four little kids too scared to matter, and—under a strawstack of curls—

Elsie Rawley, who could say verses with gestures like an actress but couldn't remember the words. Lena's eyes flicked over the line and settled on her real opponent. Winslow Starnes stared back at her with his big tan-colored eyes. He had on a yellow striped shirt with a squeezing collar not much whiter than his tow-blond hair. She had never seen him in long pants before. He looked as if he might win this contest and go right on to run for president—if they took twelve-year-olds.

Lena eased in at the opposite end of the line, by the wall, and looked out at the roomful of people. The whole congregation was there, it seemed like, and new faces that might be relatives or friends of the contestants. Mr. and Mrs. Doans, her teachers, had come in from the teacherage behind the schoolhouse. Most of the kids from school were there, too, propped against the wall or wedged in beside their folks at the too-small desks. The crowded room took her breath away. She looked out the window at the calm dusk and tried to believe she would win.

"All right," Jaybird Kelsey said suddenly. "I think it's right and fitting that we start with the high-honor student and best memorizer in Bethel Springs." He rapped the desk top with Mr. Doans's ruler. "Winslow Starnes, begin."

Winslow smiled, and in his deep, earnest voice said, "In the beginning God created the heaven and the earth." It sent a chill down Lena's backbone. He sounded like he was liable to go right through Genesis without a hitch.

The little kids came next, with "Judge not, that ye be not judged," said the other short easy ones, and Elsie said the first verse of the Twenty-third Psalm with a soft smile like a lamb.

Then everybody looked at Lena, smiling behind their eyes because she was different and comical-looking, oozing like dark dough over the edges of her last-year's Sunday dress. She took a deep breath and said softly, "God hath chosen the foolish things of the world to confound the wise; and God hath chosen the weak things

4

of the world to confound the things which are mighty."

The faces still smiled, and she thought, Wait and see, all of you. She gave Winslow a curt nod, and he started the second round. "And the earth was without form, and void—" When he got to, "And the Spirit of God moved upon the face of the waters," she was caught up by a kind of awe, thinking of the stock tank at home alive with the unearthly light of evening. But why hadn't she learned Genesis straight through, too, instead of picking the verses she liked?

They went around three times. Each time someone recited, Jaybird Kelsey made a mark beside the name on his sheet of paper. When they went around the fifth time, she saw him make a slant line through the four marks and give Winslow a glance that said, It's just a matter of time, now, boy. Lena realized that to everyone watching it wasn't a real test of who could say the most verses—it was a game to see who could hold out longest against Winslow Starnes. Even Claudie had known that and had tried to tell her.

They were waiting. She said, "Faith is the substance of things hoped for, the evidence of things not seen." Because she was going to win. They would never laugh at her again or eye her funny clothes, because they would be thinking of her Magic Mind, her amazing memory.

They went around six more times, and two of the little ones dropped out, struck mute by a contagious loss of memory. Any other time, seeing it happen like that would have frightened her, but she wasn't going to be struck blank. She was going to win. Papa would look straight at her, proud. Not the way he did now, tired and quick as if there were no need to really see her because she was like she had always been. When she won, he would see how she really was, how grown-up and—well, different now.

At the next round, the third little one dropped out. Two rounds later the last one gave up, and that left Elsie Rawley and Winslow Starnes and Lena standing alone before all the waiting faces.

Winslow switched from Genesis at the evening and

morning of the third day, and jumped to Isaiah, to Lena's relief—the swords-into-plowshares ones that her father liked. It reminded her of *The wolf shall dwell with the lamb* and *Though your sins be as scarlet,* and she felt safe and strong. Each new verse slipped easily into the space left by the last, like drawing well water, bucket after bucket.

Then without warning, Elsie Rawley stopped right in the middle of "Whatsoever things are true, whatsoever things are honest—" and couldn't finish. She looked at Lena. Lena felt her lips start to form the words, "Whatsoever things are just," but she smoothed the words away, because that wasn't the way to win. So Elsie went back into the audience, with her chin wiggling a little in disappointment. Lena looked at Winslow, and he stared back with a relieved smile that said he was glad the preliminaries were over and the real fight could begin. She looked at Papa and Claudie, and they smiled back at her from the last row of seats. The baby had gone to sleep in Claudie's lap, hanging over limply like an untrimmed pie crust, and Papa held Armilla. Roy was sitting with his neck stretched tall to see over the people in front of him.

She wished Papa had bathed. He had said it was bad enough to stop work two hours early on a Saturday, much less getting all cleaned up. But the cotton-gin dust had whitened his dark clothes and face, and people would notice when she won and Papa stood up to smile and shake hands with everybody.

She and Winslow began in earnest, using their hoarded ammunition carefully. They lingered in Ecclesiastes with *The race is not to the swift,* and *Remember now thy Creator,* and then, hesitantly, because it was beautiful and hard to understand, Lena moved into the New Testament, saying, "If ye love me, keep my commandments."

To her surprise, Winslow followed with the next verse, "And I will pray the Father, and he shall give you another Comforter, that he may abide with you forever."

She said the next verse and he answered again with the next, and she said, "Yet a little while, and the world seeth me no more; but ye see me: because I live, ye shall live also."

"At that day ye shall know that I am in my Father, and ye in me, and I in you."

There was a hush, and then a spatter of applause. They had said it well together, without stumbling, and she would have liked to smile at Winslow, but he looked away. She felt strange, saying those words she didn't understand. They seemed too large for her small mind, and she felt shy, exposed in her ignorance.

They went on, but slower now, making sure they didn't repeat a verse that had been said. Once when Winslow hesitated, and changed a line, Jaybird Kelsey questioned the preacher in a whisper, and motioned for him to go on. Lena saw the little, glassy beads of sweat come out on Winslow's forehead, and she smiled inside.

At the back of the room Papa was sitting with his feet in the aisle. His hands perched excitedly on his knees like spiders about to jump. His eyes had lighted up in his long face. Claudie watched intently, weighed down now by the heavy heads of the other two children. From Lena's new distance they looked anxious, burdened by something.

I'll show you, she said in her heart to them. I'll make you proud. And looking straight at them, she recited, "They that wait upon the Lord shall renew their strength; they shall mount up with wings as eagles; they shall run, and not be weary; and they shall walk, and not faint."

That was the one Papa said sometimes under his breath while he walked the team home from the patch at sundown. It had seemed odd at first, watching his lips move in the comforting words. But that was before she found out that Papa had meant to make a preacher when he was young.

Claudie had told her—how he had gone to a school when he had lived back South, and had to quit and go back to the farm when Granpa died. He had married

Lena's mother then, and his life had taken off in other directions, and all that was left of his dream were the words he said softly to himself in the evenings.

That was when she began memorizing verses, back in Scattercreek, as if that were something she could do to make it up to Papa. She would say them shyly after supper, watching Papa's eyes go away into a secret place, while Claudie moved around the kitchen pretending she wasn't listening but correcting a word sharply if Lena said it wrong. On cold days, on the woodbox behind the stove, she would read and memorize, warm with the rich taste of the words, and at night in cotton-picking time, when she lay rigid with fatigue, she would say them over with her lips like Papa did—the pretty ones and the Don't-be-afraid-Lena, God-is-near ones that made her taut muscles loosen their grip and lower her into sleep.

Winslow was picking from the Sermon on the Mount. She followed him, verse after verse, through the Beatitudes and *Let your light so shine,* and on, skipping, to *Consider the lilies.*

Finally he began to pause before each verse, and his hesitations made her more nervous than if they had been her own. Once, just as she started to speak, Mr. Doans's big slab of a cat jumped up into the window and looked in at her with a white beard of milk under its chin. It was twice the size of their cat—fat as she was with a litter coming—and it scared every last word out of her mind. For just a second she was sure she saw the little hungry face of Sammy Haney slide through the light and she wondered why he hadn't come inside. But she felt Jaybird Kelsey waiting hopefully with his pencil raised, and she stammered out, "For many are called, but f-few are chosen," and the battle went on.

Suddenly Jaybird Kelsey rose up just as Winslow finished a verse, and said, "Brothers and sisters, that was fifty verses for Winslow Starnes. Let's give him a big hand."

Everybody clapped encouragingly while Lena flashed with anger, waiting to say her fiftieth verse. Mr. Kelsey couldn't be faulted for appreciating spry brains, but he could save his breath, because she meant to say more verses than Winslow Starnes if he said five hundred.

In the silence that followed, she said distinctly, "Eye for eye, tooth for tooth, hand for hand, foot for foot—"

Somebody burst out laughing. There were stifled titters all over the room, and the applause pattered again for Lena's fiftieth verse, and Jaybird Kelsey ducked his head, embarrassed. But he laughed too.

They went five more rounds. Winslow stopped in the middle of a verse, strained to remember, and changed to another one.

Everyone looked at Mr. Kelsey, their eyes asking, Is that fair? He looked at the preacher. The preacher got up slowly, adjusted his cuffs, and said, "Winslow, Lena, you've each said fifty-five verses. You are beautifully matched—no one could call it anything but a perfect tie, if you would like to stop. It has been a fine and inspiring evening for every one of us. Now if you'd like—"

"I want to go on," Lena said. She hadn't come this far to be half of a perfect tie. Winslow's eyes darted at her resentfully, and slid away.

"All right." The preacher fixed his cuffs again. "May the best one win."

The crowd edged forward expectantly. Lena put her wet hands behind her and wiped them on the mashed gathers of her dress.

Two

THEY WENT FOUR MORE ROUNDS, Lena and Winslow, each thinking desperately while the other recited. For moments at a time she would find her mind blank, gleaned of its last memory, and then the strong clean words would flash back, sharp as pictures. But they came slower and harder.

Finally she felt words waiting at a distance while she stood silent, and she began slowly, "I am black, but comely, O ye daughters of Jerusalem, as the tents of Kedar, as the curtains of Solomon." She had not meant to say them. No one at home knew she had those verses from the Song of Solomon by heart. They were the ones she whispered to herself, off in the long, empty fields. "I am the rose of Sharon, and the lily of the valleys—"

While she whispered them, she was beautiful, thin as a flower, blooming with the hope of love. At those moments the years parted, and she saw her place in the world waiting to be filled. She had a house with twenty windows, and a lap robe for her buggy with a hunting scene woven in it, and pet ducks for her children. But now she was saying her dreams before all those people, saying herself to them because she had to win, and be somebody.

Winslow jumped to Revelation. She went on, verse after verse of the Song, unable to change because everything else had gone out of her head.

Then, unbelievably, Winslow's turn came, and he stood looking at Jaybird Kelsey, showing his teeth in a sad, careful smile.

Lena felt herself coiling tight inside with excitement. Jaybird Kelsey stood up uncertainly. "Winslow?" he asked.

"Yessir?" Winslow said, startled, as if that would release another verse into his mind.

"Are you stuck, boy?"

"Just for a minute," Winslow said. "Let her say one, and then I'll say two."

Mr. Kelsey studied the idea. "Does that suit you, Miss Lena?"

She glanced at Winslow, too tight with excitement to feel pity for his struggle. For an answer she said, "My beloved spake, and said unto me, Rise up, my love, my fair one, and come away."

Winslow chewed his lip, and Mr. Kelsey waited, and the crowd waited, leaning forward, and she heard her heart ticking the moments away.

When she had waited long enough for him to speak up, if he meant to, she went on, "For, lo, the winter is past, the rain is over and gone."

She waited again. Winslow lifted his hand, groping for the line he wanted. He said, "The—the time of the singing of birds—"

"No," Lena said. "The flowers appear on the earth; the time of the singing of birds is come, and the voice of the turtle is heard in our land."

She waited. Slowly Winslow's hand dropped down to his side.

She smiled, and said, "The fig tree putteth forth her green figs, and the vines with the tender grape give a good smell. Arise my love, my fair one, and come away."

She stopped. She had ruined it, and it would never mean again what it had meant when she had begged, Who will ever love me? in the lonely nights. But she was four verses ahead of him. Four verses out of herself had shown him, and everybody. She looked around dizzily and saw hands clapping, flutter flutter, all around her, and she knew she had won.

Jaybird Kelsey came to her and looked over her head. "Well, now, Miss Lena." He shifted uneasily until the clapping stopped, twitching his frizzled whiskers. He said, "Well, Miss Lena, you did real fine." He turned away. "And Winslow did fine too. Even if Winslow didn't win." He laughed, so everyone would know he had made a pun, and whacked Winslow on the back to ease the sting of defeat. He turned back to Lena with something bothersome on his mind. "Well," he said, laughing again, "we had a prize here . . ." He took a paper-wrapped package from his sagging pocket and looked at it as if he were sorry he had found it. "You win the prize, Miss Lena." He handed it out abruptly. "I wish it could have been just what you wanted, because you deserve . . ." Then he sat down as if *his* memory had failed *him* too.

Lena held it in her trembling hand and said, "Thank you, Mr. Kelsey." She unwrapped the paper.

Inside was a tie, a blue bow tie with a little celluloid hook at the back that was supposed to fit over a collar button. A boy's prize.

She looked up, surrounded. People were gawking and smiling, and she saw Winslow walk away to join Elsie Rawley as if he hadn't lost at all. She felt herself winding tighter and tighter the way a clock would until its insides burst and the hands flew off, breaking the glass front into splinters.

She wanted to yell out, "But I haven't *won* yet!" Not really won, because the reward didn't admit she had won. The ache in her happiness was like the weight of herself when she took second helpings of potatoes and cornbread at meals, too hungry to want to be thin and pretty like other girls. This wasn't the summit that winning should be. This was just holding Winslow's prize while the closing-in faces grinned at her, blocking her off from the door and the wagon and the safety of home.

"I don't want it," she said. She let it drop to the desk.

Then she saw Papa coming, with Roy asleep on his shoulder, and Claudie beside him, and she pushed toward them frantically, before she began to cry in front of all those people.

Somehow she was outside, crushed in the slow current of the crowd, with Papa's hand on her shoulder, and she caught the breath she had been holding and knew she wouldn't cry. In just a minute she might even laugh. At the silence that had dropped when she dropped the tie. At Jaybird Kelsey's confounded face. But she wouldn't cry.

Papa put the sleepy children in the back on the blanket, and Lena started to crawl up beside them. But Claudie said, "Looks to me like the winner ought to ride on the seat with Papa," and Claudie got into the back of the wagon.

Lena stood numb, until Papa took her arm and helped her up beside him.

"Well, now," he said softly.

They jolted out of the schoolhouse yard in the moonlight. She ached for him to comfort her some way. Lash out at Jaybird Kelsey for choosing a prize for the one he thought would win; tell her she was right to refuse it. But he just drove along humped over the reins. Had she embarrassed him? Was he angry, ashamed of her manners?

Maybe he thought she was happy, and he didn't want to spoil it by rebuking her. She had won and she should have been happy. Even gracious enough to take that poor little prize. Why hadn't she? She could have put it away clean and new, and someday she could have given it to her little boy; she could have knelt, laughing about tonight, pretty in a dress with lace, and given it to her little boy.

Papa. Look at me. Say something.

She couldn't breathe, sitting beside him, not knowing what he felt. She was afraid she had made him sad,

13

saying the Song of Solomon like that, revealing before all those strangers that her life lacked something. She couldn't explain that she really didn't lack anything. There was always plenty of food, and the work wasn't hard, and she had the beautiful words and the dreams, and it wasn't his fault that she longed for so many things the way she did. She didn't want him to be sad, but she couldn't explain.

Quietly, he said, "Rewards don't prove you're somebody, Lena. When you're somebody inside yourself, you don't need to be told."

She swallowed. "How do you know if you are?"

"You just know. I'm somebody, and I know."

They creaked along again for a long time, silent, and the moon rode along as unblinking as Lena.

But it was for you, she ached to tell him. You were the only prize I really wanted. You proud of me.

She was old enough not to need him so much anymore, but she did. She needed him to tell her things, and approve of her, and notice her changes. It was hard to admit, but true, and she knew it.

She didn't think he knew it, though.

Papa said, "You didn't have to throw Mr. Kelsey's blunder up to him, Lena."

"It was meant for Winslow Starnes," she flared. "He can have it."

"But you had the victory," Papa reminded her. "Wasn't that enough?"

No, she thought wearily, you're giving me the wrong prize, too, Papa. Can't you say I did good?

She sat silent beside him the rest of the way home.

Each of them carried a sleeping child into the dark house. The baby woke as Lena put him down into his banana-box cradle, and Claudie closed herself into the bedroom with him to nurse him back to sleep. Papa went out again to unhitch the team. Sleepily, Lena fumbled for a match to light the kitchen lamp. The room's gray shapes flickered and steadied in the yellow glow.

As she adjusted the wick, a little breath of strangeness blew across her neck. Something was wrong. Something had changed while they were gone. Then she saw

14

what it was, right in front of her, and her hand froze holding the dead match. Claudie had baked bread that afternoon and left the loaves to cool on the table with a cloth over them. They sat just as they had, but someone had stabbed Claudie's butcher knife through one of the loaves, cloth and all, and left it there.

Lena jerked backward two steps, crying, "Claudie!" and whirled to search the room's shadows for whatever else might leap at her.

Claudie opened the door and stared at the knife pinning its black shadow to the cloth. "Lord help us," she whispered. "Call your daddy." She seized the lamp and went into the lean-to room that Lena shared with Roy and Armilla. She knelt and looked under the beds. The children stirred and slept on as she shut the door.

Papa came at a run, and stared the way Claudie had. His face sagged. "Is that all?" he asked between breaths. His eyes darted everywhere. He eased the door shut and let down the latch that they never used.

"Is that *all?*" Claudie repeated in a changed voice. "Does it have to be stuck in you before you see what it means?" She was shivering.

Papa came and put his arm around her, saying, "Hush, now," but she pulled away.

"Ben, it's happening like it always does."

"What is? What's happening?" Lena asked, big-eyed.

"Nothing," Papa said quietly. "Just some kid dared another one to sneak in here, and he left this to prove how brave he was."

"Ben," Claudie said.

"Or a tramp was scared off by something just when he was fixing to have some supper—"

"Ben! They're telling us. They don't want us here."

"Who?" Lena asked.

"They're saying we're a threat to them, Ben. They're saying here out west they don't have any more use for us than they did back South. We never should have come."

"Who's saying?" They were talking past her as if she were part of the furniture.

"Tonight she pushed a white town too fast, Ben—

15

she overstepped herself just like you're always doing!"

Papa looked straight at Claudie and said in a cold voice, "Be quiet."

Her eyes blazed back into his. "I been quiet. Six years while she was growing up safe in Scattercreek, and you not telling her what the rest of the world was like. Or letting me."

"There's a right time," Papa said.

"Well, when? Tonight you knew what might happen, but you said, Oh they like us here we're not any different from them out here, and I stayed quiet while she won over a white boy, and you still hadn't told her what she needs to know!"

She pushed past Lena into the bedroom and slammed the door.

The lamplight wavered on the water bucket and Papa's shaving mirror, and went still. They stood without moving, as though her words had thrown a spell. Papa went over and started to draw the knife out of the bread. Its blade had gone through into the table. He worked it free and put it back into the drawer. As it slid out of sight, his eyes closed.

Lena gazed at the slit in the cloth. "Papa." Her own voice startled her. "Was I not supposed to win?"

He opened his eyes and smiled at her. "I'm glad you won. You won fair."

"But, Papa. Did somebody do this because I won?" Suddenly she was freezing. Tremors of coldness shook her.

Papa sat down at the table and held out his hand to her. She came and let him draw her down onto his knees. It had been years since he had done that.

"I'm too big, Papa," she said awkwardly.

"I remember when I used to hold you on my lap. Your little feet about the size of a mouse. Curly-toed."

She waited, feeling his knee-bones braced to hold her weight.

"Nobody did this because you won tonight, Lena."

"But Claudie said—"

"I know. She said what she thought was true. What

16

is true for her." She felt him sigh, deeply, like someone who had run a long time and had stopped to draw breath. "She's right, there's things I haven't told you. I hoped I wouldn't have to. And some things I never will, because they're past and ought to be put out of our memory to give room for better things."

"Papa, do people want us to leave?"

He sighed again, and curved her cold hand into his. "No. This is a good town we've come to. You know that—they took us in: the church, the school. This is big, open country with room for everybody."

"But somebody came in here tonight."

"I know. But maybe just somebody young. Or angry. Or scared of changes."

In a flash of memory she saw Tater Haney sitting on his daddy's horse, his face carved into a long stare.

"But one person, or two, or ten, they're not a whole town," Papa said. "We lived in Scattercreek because it's a fact some towns back there don't want black people and won't let them in. So black people balance that by making their own communities like Scattercreek, with their own schools and churches and stores. It eases some of the trouble. But we're American citizens with the right to live in any town."

"What trouble? What did Claudie mean, right at first? About—about a knife in you?"

He was silent, trying to decide what to say. "You were a baby when we lived back South, Lena, so you don't remember; you don't understand how things were, sometimes." She could smell the dust of cotton linters on his clothes, the faint scent of crushed burs like fresh corn. "Things happened to folks there that left scars on Claudie, and make her afraid they'll happen again. She felt safe when we moved to Scattercreek. But now she's way out here because I came, I wanted more for all of us than Scattercreek. Now she's an outsider, lonesome, and a happening like this, tonight, seems bigger than it is." He eased her off his knees and turned her to face him. "I don't want this to worry you, little Lena. We haven't done anything wrong, and we don't

17

have anything to be scared about. What we want to remember about this night is that you did a wonderful thing and made us proud. You won."

He was smiling, still holding her hands hard in his, and she tried to smile back. He had said it, finally. But all the other things he had said rolled over it like a storm in her mind. Through its darkness, like lightning, flashed the pale face of Sammy Haney peeking past the Doans's cat in the schoolhouse window. She threw her arms around Papa, prickling with dread.

"Papa, I think I know who came in."

He squeezed her close. "I think you do too," he said, sadly as if he were sorry.

She was astonished. "What can we do?"

"Well, we can go to bed."

He led her to the door of the lean-to. She started to go in, and couldn't. A whole herd of questions broke through her fenced-up distress. "Papa, why would Tater Haney hate us? We haven't done anything to him. What gives him the right? He wasn't even there tonight when I won—I didn't win from *him*. Papa, is it wrong to want to be better than other people?"

He stood with his hand on the china doorknob. She could hear his slow breathing as he hunted for the right answer. He said, "Nobody's better than anybody else. The Lord has a special need for all of us, or we wouldn't be here. But the thing you want to strive for, always, is to be better than yourself. And we all fall short on that." Then he shut the door.

When she lay rigid under her quilt, listening to the little kids' dream-mumbles in the other bed, she tried to understand what he meant. But her mind kept filling with the picture of a neat, small knife-slit in a white cloth that looked like Papa's shirt.

 Three

NO ONE CALLED Lena the next morning, and the Sunday sun was already warming her face when she woke. Roy and Armilla were two patchwork hills in the other bed. With their eyes closed, Papa's eyes, they had Claudie's calm look, her strong, beautiful cheekbones. She wondered if they looked like their mother because they had her there to copy somehow, as they grew and took shape. Then how was Lena going to know who to be?

She had been nearly three, as young as Armilla, when her real mother, her model, had gone out of her life. By the time she was five, like Roy, Claudie was her new mother, and in between was a blur of granmas and aunts and changing rooms and the scary feel of new towns. Through it all, the only constant face was Papa's. She guessed she looked like Papa.

They were talking in the kitchen, their murmuring voices the same as every morning, the coffee's bitter fragrance the same, as if nothing had happened last night. Maybe nothing had, and she had dreamed it.

But it was Sunday—had they forgotten? She scooted

out of bed and ran in, still in her nightgown, exclaiming, "Won't we be late for church?"

Claudie was taking out biscuits. She looked at Papa, and he said, "We thought we'd skip today and let everybody sleep." He sat down at the table and put his plate in the empty space where the loaves of bread had sat.

Lena glanced quickly at their faces. They looked tired, but they had that calm, talked-through look they sometimes had, mornings after they had disagreed on something—a together look that calmed her, too. What had happened slid into perspective, an incident, almost funny. Tater Haney showing off in an empty house, while his little brother scouted for him to be sure no one came home and interrupted his bravery.

She made an unexpected sniff of relief, and Papa looked up questioningly. Claudie said, "She thinking, if we don't go to church, she going to pile that cat in her lap and sit out there on that sunny stoop till she memorizes two thousand more Bible verses." She was trying so hard to jolly everybody up, after what she had said last night, that Lena laughed for her.

It was true, there was nothing she would rather do on her day of rest. But it would have to wait until after the little kids were dressed and fed, and the kitchen cleaned, and water and wood brought in, and the beans looked through for rocks and put on to simmer. Not to mention her arithmetic lesson for tomorrow.

She fell into gloom, and poured syrup over her biscuit, trying to make the slow brown dribble spell her name. At least she wasn't the only one with chores. Besides his regular farm work and his Saturdays at the gin, Papa had the team and pigs and Mrs. Chism's cow to look after. He carried half the milk up to Mrs. Chism every morning, sometimes taking along the linens Claudie had ironed for her; the flat stuff, not the ruffled clothes, which Claudie ironed right in Mrs. Chism's kitchen so that they could go straight into the closet without a wrinkle. And its being Sunday didn't exempt Claudie from cooking, and carrying water to the last of her drying-up garden, boiling the rag squares that the baby dirtied every day.

Papa got up, hesitating a moment before he scraped his plate into Bullet's pan. Lena wondered why she hadn't heard the old dog thumping stiffly as he waited at the door. Off exploring on the river, maybe, or over at the prairie-dog town. Papa took something from the pocket of his coat hanging behind the door and handed it to Lena. Her face lit up. It was a newspaper—columns of captured thoughts, people, happenings. Magic. She would sit all day and devour it line by line.

"Miss Chism gave me a pile of peach seeds to plant, and they were wrapped in this," Papa said, thumping the front page. "September twelve, nineteen ten—not a month old."

Lena had already disappeared into the newspaper. Theodore Roosevelt's New Nationalism speech in Kansas augured ill for President Taft, whatever that meant. In the next column, a fat black advertisement proclaimed that Dr. Hustletter's Trusses were the Medical Triumph of the Age.

"Miss Chism wants you to come help her tomorrow," Papa said.

Lena's eyes appeared at the top of the paper. He couldn't mean her. Tomorrow was school—the day she would smile benignly into the faces saying silently or aloud, You did good!—the day Mrs. Doans would say, Well, here is our Lena.

"She wants to put up her tomatoes before a frost gets them," Papa said, "and clean up for a big dinner she's fixing to give next Sunday." Lena's lips started to form a but-Papa. He lifted his hand to stop it. "You do her a good job."

"Yessir," Lena said tightly.

She had never worked for Mrs. Chism. The idea set her stomach churning. She had gone once with Claudie just after they had moved into Mrs. Chism's rent-house in May. Claudie had taken the baby because he was sick, and had taken Lena to watch Brother while she ironed. Lena had held him, outside under a hackberry tree all day, on orders from Mrs. Chism, who wasn't about to risk a sick baby's throwing up on her rug. The only nice thing about Mrs. Chism's was her old bulldog,

21

Lulu, popeyed, fat and stone-deaf, who had shared the hackberry shade with them. Brother and Lulu had nearly loved each other to death. Which was more than she could say for Claudie and Mrs. Chism that day.

Papa said, "Go by and tell your teacher why you can't come. Find out what you'll be missing, so you can study it at night and keep up."

Lena rolled her eyes to show fortitude, and nodded. The paper said the Russians were in constant dread of further moves by Austria. "Papa, is Russia going to have a war?"

"I hope not."

"If we had a war over here, would you fight in it?"

"I don't know," Papa said slowly.

"Papa! You wouldn't be scared, would you?"

"I don't think killing people is any way to solve problems."

Claudie said, "If they took you, it would be so you could shovel their manure and haul their freight, not kill people."

Papa smiled. "You sound like I'd have to miss the best part. Just the same, they had black soldiers in the Revolution, and in the Civil War too. Even with Colonel Roosevelt down in Cuba in ninety-eight."

"They did?" Lena asked in surprise. It didn't say that in her history book. But she was born in ninety-eight, and it didn't say that either.

"I'm talking about now," Claudie said. From the way she looked at Papa, what had happened last night was not finished between them.

"Well, I'm talking about anytime," Papa said. "Killing is wrong. The Lord commanded, 'Thou shalt not kill.'"

"But Papa, in the very next chapter Moses says anybody that smited a man and killed him shall surely die."

"Right there in Exodus," Claudie said, moving up like a second cannon to reinforce Lena. "Eye for eye."

"Wrong just the same." Papa stared down their muzzles. "'Be not overcome by evil, but overcome evil with good.'" His look could have melted cannonballs. "'Vengeance is mine; *I* will repay, saith the Lord.' So

22

they'll just have to fight their war over in Europe without me. I've got cotton sacks to patch."

He started toward the door, but Claudie laid her hand on his arm. "Tell her, Ben."

Papa gazed past her at the newspaper in Lena's lap, as if reading it might show him how to answer her.

"Ben," Claudie said, "the hoping time is over again. Tell her, or I'll tell her my way, whether you like it or not."

Hoping time? Over *again?* Lena gaped from one to the other. Nothing made sense. Neither did her father's face, fixed halfway between anger and grief.

"Take her down to the trees," Claudie said, softly, because she was winning.

Papa gave Lena's nightgown a little tweak. She went into the lean-to and skinned into her regular dress.

They went outside, and looked at the stretching distance. They lived on the ridge where river-bottom farmland gave way to drier, poorer grazing range. Far away, two mounds like ears broke the horizon. Nothing else made a jag in the level line that separated land from sky.

"What's at the trees?" Lena asked. She could see them, summer-dingy cottonwoods, edging the river like watchers at a parade.

Papa began to walk toward them. His stiff, worn shoes clumped on the packed earth of the yard. His steps softened as he climbed through the barbed wire fence and started across the pasture grass. Lena followed. The house shrank against the sky, raw and unprotected, gnawed by the wind. In the distance, set apart on their acreages, were other houses, their gray boards bleached and warped, too, by years of enduring.

"What does Claudie want you to tell me, Papa?" His silence made her more apprehensive than hearing something terrible would have. She could see Mrs. Chism's busy-roofed house sitting high on the river bluff in a ruffle of trees, and her stomach churned again.

"Well, she thinks I've got forty years of history that belongs to you and I haven't given it to you. How am I going to give it to you?" He began to take long strides as if he were hurrying to catch all that time streaming backward out of his reach. "When I was born, my daddy had been a freedman for five years. Not property. Nobody owned him—or his children. Do you understand what that meant?"

"I think so," Lena said, puffing to keep up.

"When I was eight, my daddy took us all to Kansas. Forty, fifty thousand black people went. It was like Moses leading his people to the land of freedom. They called us Exodusters. It was clean and big out there, and Kansas folks said they'd fought to be a free state and it was fitting for us to be there."

"But you didn't stay," Lena said.

"No. That winter we froze in sunny Kansas. There got to be too many of us, white people said, and why didn't we go to Liberia where we belonged?" Papa snatched the heads off the sunflowers they were walking through. "My little sisters died from the flux. My daddy lost his land. So he packed us up and went back South." He slung the flower heads as hard as he could. "If he could just have had the money to get started. Lord, if he could just have stuck it out."

That must have been when Papa promised himself he'd try again to go west. She could tell by his face.

"Was that the hoping time, Papa? That's over again?"

Beyond Mrs. Chism's house she could see the town in a smudge of smoke and dust. Once Papa had asked her, "Do you know what Bethel means? It means the house of God. A hallowed spot."

"It was all a hoping time. Even during the war—all those people fighting for our rights. Then when it ended, and black people actually began to read and write and own property and have a say in making the laws—can you imagine it? All that promise? All the things they could see ahead for their children?"

She watched in silence as the light went out of his face, his body, the way a cloud shadow slides across a field.

"But it didn't happen. I ask myself, how could it *not* happen? I lived through it, Lena. In my lifetime we went back into the dirt again, back there in the South. They reconstructed us—one little loss at a time. We could

24

vote at first, and now we can't. We could go anywhere, and now we sit in the back of the trains and live in darktowns and swear on a different Bible in court so white witnesses won't have to touch the same holy words we touch."

She stumbled along behind him. His back was like a stranger's. It shocked her to hear him expose the pain hiding beneath his loving-kindness. She wished he would stop, but she knew he couldn't, and she couldn't let him. This was part of her life too.

"Somehow we got put in our place again. Belittled. Threatened. Lynched. Denied. That's the part Claudie wanted you to know. Men hanging from trees. Children being taught every day that God meant them to be inferior. That's why we moved to Scattercreek, so our children could be spared that, we thought."

Lena could feel the "we" of her past, her people, become the "we" of her family now, a tiny chip flying off from the whole.

"It was easier there," Papa said, "but I wasn't proud of myself. So we gathered up our courage and moved on, out west here. That was our hoping time, our little Exodus. The promised land, where people would look at us and see *us,* not our color. Last night you stood up there, the equal of any person in the world, because you were good at something, you had worked till you excelled. That was a proud moment."

"And then, when we got home."

He nodded. "That little reminder. Just to say we hadn't run far enough. Just to say somebody, even out here, can't accept the fact of us. Claudie cried last night. She asked to go back to Scattercreek."

"I won't go," Lena said.

"Maybe we should," Papa said. They were at the trees.

"No—I won't. Papa, you can't either!" She was appalled. "You said last night—we haven't done anything to be afraid of, or ashamed of. If you believe that, then we have to stay."

Papa stopped beside a fallen cottonwood. Its roots had torn a hole in the loose river-bottom soil as they pulled away, and someone had filled it up again by scraping sand into it with an old board.

"Bullet's there," Papa said.

She stared at the still-fresh mound.

"I found him this morning when I was taking the milk to Miss Chism."

Her tongue was too thick to move. Finally she said, "What happened to him?"

"I don't know for sure. Animals want to die alone, it's their nature. So he came out here, and I buried him."

"But he was all right yesterday!" She saw him in the road, his tail sweeping in farewell as they left him behind. "Did he have a fight?"

"I can't say. More like he had been hit, or poisoned."

"Tater? It was Tater, wasn't it?"

Papa looked down sternly at her. "You can't say that, Lena, because we don't know."

"I do know. I just know. Papa, can't we tell the sheriff?"

"Lena, I showed you because I didn't want to lie to you and say Bullet just wandered off and never came back. Claudie would have told you the truth anyway. But the truth is—I found him dead this morning. That's all. That's the way we have to leave it."

She opened her mouth, but the look on his face stopped her first word. She turned away. The trees blurred. She picked up a marbled rock worn smooth on its long journey from some faraway home, and pushed it gently into the center of the mound. Then she started back across the pasture.

Papa walked in silence behind her. She wished he would put his hand on her shoulder and scatter all her confusion and pain. But she knew that if he did she would twitch her shoulder out from under his fingers and walk on faster.

It felt strange to be angry at Papa for not letting her hate Tater Haney. She did hate him, in spite of Papa. Tater the most. Then Sammy because he must have known about and even helped in what happened. Then the rest of the Haneys who had let it happen. She hated them all—everyone involved.

The idea startled her. It had not occurred to her that other people might have known, and sent Tater off to do what they would have done if they had dared. How many smiles last night might have been masking secrets? She thought, That's why we didn't go to church today. We would have looked at all those faces, and wondered . . .

As if he had looked into her mind, Papa said, "I want you to behave exactly like you always have, Lena. In school. In town. I expect you to be civil. To Tater's little brother. Everybody. It's not your place to judge people. That's for God. Do you hear me?"

She broke into a run that scattered grasshoppers. The coarse sunflower leaves slashed at her legs. She could see the windmill at home, fluttering like some kind of gaunt, tethered bird. Then the house, frozen on its skinny brick stilts like a fat lady who had seen a mouse. She had the wild idea of running right past it, never stopping, until she disappeared between the two little mounds on the horizon.

Or maybe she would climb them. She would like to know why the Comanches had called them medicine hills when they lived there, and what their medicine could cure.

When she looked back, Papa had stopped and was staring across Mrs. Chism's field. The shocks of feed propped together made an Indian village of little tepees.

She slowed to a walk, regretting that she hadn't answered him. She didn't know what had come over her. Except that last night her nice tick-tocking life had stopped.

As she crawled through the fence into the yard, Roy came bounding off the porch. Each time his feet hit the ground a word popped out of him. Finally she could make it out. "Kitties," he was calling. "Kitties. Kitties."

He was a skinny wiggle of importance as he grabbed her hand and urged her up the porch steps. Claudie sat on the top step beside a washtub. Armilla hung over its edge so far that only Claudie's hand on the tail of her dress kept her from toppling in on her head.

Claudie said, "The family grew while you were gone."

The mama-cat was in the tub on a bed of rags, briskly cleaning her four new children. Lena knelt down into the smell of wet wool. They were beginning to dry off—three soft gray babies and one black one. They bumbled blindly across their mother's legs, lifting little mashed-in faces with hanging-down ears. Tweets of sound came out of them as they hunted for their dinner.

"Don't touch," Claudie warned Armilla as her little hand reached down to feel.

Roy was grinning as if he had invented cats. "What they names?" he kept asking. He had biscuit crumbs in his hair.

"They don't have names yet," Claudie said, looking over his head at Papa coming across the pasture. "Go bring that pan of scraps out here, I bet this old mama's hungry." Even the cat had no name. It had been there when they moved in, left by the last tenants, and they had called it Cat as if they somehow had no right to rename it for themselves.

Roy came out with the scraps that would have been for Bullet. Lena gave a shudder of surrender and began to cry.

Claudie leaned and put her arm around her. "You sad about that old dog."

Lena nodded and then shook her head. "Yes, but—" She didn't know how to say it. Her tears dropped onto the mama-cat's fur. "Why won't Papa stand up to them? Is he scared of everybody? He let that old crabby lady just look in his direction, Yes ma'am, no ma'am, Lena don't mind missing school. And then Bullet—"

"Well, now, hold on a minute," Claudie said. She was watching Papa go into the barn for the cotton sacks that needed sewing up. "We all work for that crabby old lady and you better not let your daddy hear you call her that."

"But why do we have to work for her and live where she tells us to?"

"She's our boss."

"Does that mean we have to let people break into our house and kill our dog and try to scare us back to Scattercreek—"

"Hush up," Claudie said sharply. Roy's eyes were as big as prunes. "I think I better set you straight, Miss Lena. Cause you don't know the first thing about what's bothering your daddy." Her calm brows had clinched together in anger. Mentioning Scattercreek had hit her wrong. "Sure, your daddy's scared."

Lena raised her head, her mouth open in amazement. She had expected Claudie to defend him. She had counted on it.

"Sure he's scared," Claudie said. "Sure he thinks about leaving. Do you know why, Miss Magic Mind? No you don't. You worrying about missing a few days of school like that made any difference, when your daddy has a life-and-death real worry to struggle with. Do you have any idea what that is?"

Lena shook her head, as wide-eyed now as Roy.

"Well, it's this. Your daddy is a good man—he believes the Lord meant it when He said to love your enemies and turn the other cheek to those that hurt you. What your daddy is struggling with in his soul right now is what he would do if somebody tried to hurt his family."

The mama-cat got out of the tub and ate the scraps Roy had put down on the porch. The kittens poked and blundered in the empty space, hunting her warmth. Slowly Lena shrank into herself, shocked and chastened by Claudie's words.

Papa was coming across the yard with the sacks. He didn't seem to be struggling. He seemed natural. Tomorrow he and Claudie would be in the field by daylight, dragging the sacks down the cotton rows. The little kids would sit with their cold bare feet buried in the cotton piled at the edge of the field, till the sun warmed up the day.

She didn't understand Papa. When picking first started, he refused to let her stay out of school to help. She didn't join them till she got home, and then they all picked till dark. But tomorrow, and for no telling how long, she would go to Mrs. Chism's big house, as if missing school didn't matter. Papa's way of thinking perplexed her. And what Claudie had said didn't make sense either. If someone tried to hurt his family, Papa wouldn't let them. That was all there was to it. Wasn't it?

He came up onto the porch and looked into the tub. His tense face relaxed in a smile. "Well, how about that?" he asked Roy. He gave Armilla's bottom a pat, because it was all he could see of her.

"What they names, Papa?" Roy demanded.

The mama-cat returned to the tub and checked her blind, bumping family. "Well, that little black devil, you better call him Old Nick," Papa said.

"There's three alike," Claudie said blandly, as if kittens were all in the world she had on her mind. "What kind of names come in threes?"

"Red, white and blue," Roy yelled.

"Lock, stock and barrel," Papa said, smiling. "Shadrach, Meshach and Abed-nego."

Claudie swatted at both of them in mock annoyance. "Pretty names for these little soft babies."

"Lena knows three good names," Papa said, looking into her face for the first time. "From one of the verses last night." His eyes were kind. He had understood the anger and confusion that had made her run from him.

Then she knew the names he meant. She picked up the first almost-fluffy mite, and guided it to the comfort of its mother's nipple. "Faith," she said softly. She lined the other two beside their sturdy black brother who had already found his dinner. "Hope. And Charity." She managed a faint smile to match Papa's.

Papa put the last of Bullet's scraps into the tub and stroked the mama-cat's head. "Something always comes to fill the empty places," he said, as she chewed thankfully. "Something comes to take the place of what you lose."

Four

THE FIRST-THROUGH-EIGHTH-GRADE kids were milling around in the yard when Lena stopped by the school the next morning on her way to Mrs. Chism's. She didn't see Sammy Haney, but his turnip was propped in the ink-well hole on his desk when she went in. Winslow and Elsie were erasing the blackboard.

"Where's teacher?" she asked.

"Storeroom," Winslow answered. He stopped erasing, and for a second, staring at her, he seemed about to say something else. But he silently watched her go into the little shed at the back of the building.

Mr. and Mrs. Doans were kneeling behind the stacks of books and firewood, patching ratholes with strips from a tin can. When she told them why she was going to be absent, Mrs. Doans took her into the schoolhouse and marked the lessons in her books so that she could keep up with the rest of her class. She was glad Winslow and Elsie were gone. She packed her books in her satchel, being careful not to mash her lunch. Claudie was almost sure Mrs. Chism would feed Lena, but to

31

be safe she had put a fried egg into a biscuit and sent it along.

Lena went on up the road to the big house, breathing short with excitement. It loomed up, its steep roof sprouting lightning rods. The famous automobile Claudie had told her about was out of sight somewhere—stored in the barn most likely. Beyond an iron fence, flowers, tired from summer, drooped along the high, granite foundation of the house. The walk led through green grass and up a flight of steps to a porch made of wooden lace. Spindles, scrolls and scallops decorated every banister and post. She had knocked and was gazing through the colored glass in the door before she remembered she should have gone around to the back.

The oval of beautiful colors flew backward and the oval of Mrs. Chism stood in its place. She almost filled the doorway. An old, jowly, sharp-eyed face looked out from between the flounced collar of a wrapper and a high, puffed switch of hair not quite the color of her own.

"Well?" she snapped.

Lena quailed and gulped. "You told my daddy you wanted me."

"I hope you're smarter than you look," Mrs. Chism said, stepping back grudgingly. She almost squashed the old deaf bulldog asleep on the flowered rug. "Well, get in here and stop gawking. I've been up since four—I don't sleep worth a damn anymore."

She turned and clomped through the grandest parlor Lena had ever seen in her life—in her dreams, to be exact, because she had never seen a real one. The chairs and sofas were green plush, tasseled and fringed at every edge. Curlicued picture frames tilted down at her, caught from falling in the nick of time by golden rope. Hundreds of glass vases and prisms and statues and lamp globes quivered as Mrs. Chism swept past in a windstorm of flounces.

"Well?" she snapped again at the kitchen door. Lena got her feet moving and sped through the parlor and dining room where a great oak table was littered with

32

breakfast dishes for one. In the kitchen she drew up short beside a bushel basket of tomatoes.

She thought she might as well die and get it over. She didn't know how to can tomatoes. She had watched neighbors back in Scattercreek, but nothing useful had stuck in her head. A box marked MASON JARS sat on the table. She knew what a mason was. A bricklayer. She couldn't lay bricks either. Out of the corner of her eye, she hunted for a door she could bolt through.

Mrs. Chism said, "When we get these here things canned and the kitchen scrubbed we're going to clear the attic out. I haven't been up there since Gooch died." The "we" gave Lena momentary comfort. She wasn't going to be left alone in that enormous kitchen to produce canned tomatoes. "Disgusting," Mrs. Chism said, eating a tomato, but whether she meant the tomato, or the late Mr. Chism, or the attic was not clear.

They set to work, and the first thing Lena did was wrong. Mrs. Chism asked for a pan of water, and had to grab Lena's flying skirt because she went running outside to get it, forgetting that the pump was right there in the kitchen. When Mrs. Chism said *hot* water, Lena started to put the kettle on, until Mrs. Chism, muttering back-of-the-barn language, showed her the reservoir at the side of the big curly stove. The mason jars were for tomatoes, not bricklayers, she discovered when she opened the box. They had to be set in a pan and scalded. Of course she banged two of them together and they both broke, and she prayed to disappear from the face of the earth. But she didn't, and by midmorning the remaining jars lined the washstand, filled with skinned red balls that looked as hot and mashed as she did.

All the time, Mrs. Chism talked. Maybe she had her first audience in ten years, Lena decided. It had been that long since she had Mr. Chism to talk to. To hear Mrs. Chism tell it, he had died trying to catch a three-thirty train at three-thirty-four.

She said, "You'd think a eighty-year-old man would a lot rather pass away politely in his own bed instead

33

of galloping down the track after a train, with the clothes flying out of his satchel all along the Katy Line. But not Gooch. He would have been ninety next month if he had caught it, barring any more crazy doings. I was twenty-seven years younger than Gooch, you have to remember, and we understood each other very satisfactory. I married him for his land, and he married me for—" She peered up into her false bangs as though she had just remembered she had them pinned on. "My looks," she finished. She had a laugh like a corn grinder. She turned it on and ground for a moment. "When you're pretty and round in all the right places, it's easy to just slide along and get round all over."

She brought a pie out of the ice box and glared at it. It had beautiful white foam like soapsuds over the top, but she couldn't have looked more disgusted if she had spied mouse tracks going across it.

"I'm fat," she said sadly, and cut a slice. Lena swallowed back a drool and went on scrubbing the tomato splotches off the floor. All at once a slice of pie appeared under her nose. "Eat," Mrs. Chism commanded. "There must be something you can do right." She surprised Lena by grinding out another short cornmealy laugh, and Lena giggled back. Without much hesitation they finished up the pie and called it early lunch.

The first thing Lena saw when she reached the attic behind Mrs. Chism was a stack of books. Then, piles of them, boxes of them, dumped like trash on the floor. "Are all these yours?" She almost whispered in admiration.

"Those? Oh, hell, I took those out of the bookcases when my kids moved away. I needed a place to store my good dishes."

"But—do you come up here to read them?" It was like seeing the pie. Her mouth watered.

In the one-window dimness Mrs. Chism stared at her with no expression on her face. "We'll start in the far corner," she said. "I'm clearing out Gooch's stuff. And the children's stuff. Selling the whole lot. If they wanted it, they should have come got it. A little visit to their own mother wouldn't kill them. I've got grandchildren I haven't even seen."

Lena backed away longingly from the books. She had to ask if she could read them. She had to read them. Even school didn't have half as many, and besides she had read those. But the time didn't seem right. Maybe after she had worked hard and the tightness had left Mrs. Chism's face . . .

They worked all afternoon in a dusty, golden light. The attic held more things than a general store. They filled boxes with clothes to sell, clothes to give to the missions, and clothes to keep till Mrs. Chism might squeeze into them again. They boxed old letters and toys and broken furniture and rusted gadgets; they packed faded curtains and rerolled rugs. "Good! I'll get Starnes over here tomorrow," Mrs. Chism said. Winslow's father ran the dry-goods store. His undertaking business was on the second floor, and at the back he sold secondhand articles.

By the time they reached the books, Lena was tingling with excitement.

"Pile them over there under the eaves somewhere," Mrs. Chism directed.

Lena drew a breath of relief. At least they were not being sold immediately with the other things. But she remembered the mouse-gnawed newspapers and rain-soaked clothes they had found under the eaves. Her courage surged up protectively. "Could I read your books, please, Miss Chism?"

Mrs. Chism set down a dress form shaped the way she must have been shaped once. "You? What good do you think books would do you?"

Lena opened her mouth and didn't know how to start. It was like being asked what good food or water or air was. You had to have them, that was all. "I learn things," she said.

"The devil you do," Mrs. Chism snorted. She grabbed two books up by their spines. *"Clarabel's Love Story. Winsome but Wicked.* That's what my daughter

35

learned. Romance. Romance. Now she lives over a saloon in Milwaukee with a one-eyed butcher. So much for romance."

"But—" Lena began. She had seen one of Mr. Dickens's books, and *The Arabian Nights*. "You have one called *Cook's Voyages around the World*. And *Grimm's Household Stories*—"

"Under the eaves," Mrs. Chism ordered.

"But please, Miss Chism. I'd—I'd work extra for borrowing them. Anything! I can't see why not, if you don't use them—"

She had gone too far. Mrs. Chism put her face down to Lena's. Her bangs bristled, and her teeth clicked. "I don't have to take sass from you, little swellhead. You've been more of a headache than you're worth, this whole day. Skid them books under the eaves right now or else start down them steps and out the door."

They glared at each other. Desperately Lena tried to decide whether to shrink a size to please Mrs. Chism, or stand tall to please herself. Which would Papa do? She saw him, smiling at her but not proud. People are afraid of changes, Lena. Remember? Don't try to push them too fast.

Under the frumpy bangs that couldn't make her look young again, Mrs. Chism's eyes wavered the tiniest bit. Maybe she knew that the books held something she lacked, with all her possessions.

Lena unfolded an old waterproof wagon sheet and stacked the books on it. She slid the long heavy bundle under the eaves.

"Good idea," Mrs. Chism said shortly. She wiped her hands. "Let's go eat."

Lena hesitated. The light was dimming into dusk.

"Oh, come on," Mrs. Chism insisted. She grumbled out a laugh. "I used to cook for a railroad crew. Baked twelve pies and ten dozen rolls a day. I still can't help cooking twenty times more food than I can eat. It won't take but a few minutes."

She creaked down the stairs and began to bang life into the kitchen stove. Lena stood at the top step. Once she had seen a wasp kill a spider and carry it, limp and curled, into its tunnel. She felt like the spider. At the foot of the stairs, her book satchel stood on the floor, still full of egg-and-biscuit and homework to do yet.

She took a long, sad breath. Then she grabbed the biggest book she could feel under the wagon sheet, plunged silently down the stairs, and slid it into her satchel.

She went in and set the table for Mrs. Chism, numbed by her own audacity. Mrs. Chism forked up pickles from her ten-gallon keg to go with the ham and leftover soup and rice and potato salad and can of shredded pineapple she had laid out. They had mail-order crackers and four tomatoes they had missed that morning, and drank wild-cherry phosphate out of cut-glass goblets. Lena ate in a kind of dream. She had never tasted pineapple, but it went down like all the rest, sawdusty with the guilt of that book bulging in her satchel.

Mrs. Chism stuffed her napkin into a ring shaped like a monkey playing a drum. Lena watched and stuffed hers into a monkey playing a banjo. Now, Lena thought, the dishes and then home. She could almost feel her legs pounding down the dark road. But Mrs. Chism flipped the table scraps off onto Lulu's waiting smashed-back nose, and said, "I eat good, don't I? My folks were dirt-poor. We lived in a chicken house one winter. I said then I was never going to be poor again, and now I've got one thousand nine hundred and twenty acres of land that says I won't." She aimed her fork at Lena. "You know what my children are doing? Sitting on their hind legs waiting for me to die, so *they* won't ever be poor again. They are going to be surprised right down to their socks. They are not going to get it. I'm going to get it. I'm going to sell off that land and spend it up, doing what I want to do and having what I want to have and eating what I want to eat."

She threw back her head and made her mechanical laugh. Lena could imagine her, alone with Lulu in that huge house, grinding her laugh-mill suddenly in the silence to see if it still worked.

"I want your daddy to ride over to my place at Hawk Hill and get those fences back in shape before I send a buyer out to look at it. That no-good Haney was supposed to mend fence last spring, but he never took his tail off the porch long enough to go do it. I'd throw the whole ratty bunch of them off my land if his old woman wasn't about to have another bug-eyed baby."

The windows were dark. They sat in twilight at a ghost-white table. Lena said, "I better wash the dishes and get home before my folks get worried."

"Oh, get on home. You can do the dishes in the morning," Mrs. Chism said.

Lena felt a surge of relief. She hadn't been fired at the end of her first day. She couldn't let herself get fired—she was helping to pay for the rent and the loaned cow and the little kids' next shoes. But the relief slid backward like a wave at the thought of another day—an endless string of days—with Mrs. Chism. The work wasn't hard—her tiredness was different from field-work tiredness. The strain came from feeling two ways about everything. It was more like being in a war without knowing for sure who was your enemy or your friend, or even what you were fighting about.

She gathered up her satchel and went out, trying to make her feet take ordinary steps. The moment she was out of view beyond a lilac hedge, she broke into a run. It was late. The wind had sunk. The lump of the book banged like an anvil against her knees.

As she sped around the corner into the main road, someone stepped out of the dark hedgerow and blocked her way. She made a squeak of alarm and whirled instinctively. Then, just as instinctively, as her mind registered whom she had seen, she whirled back and ran into Papa's arms.

She could feel him laugh. "Did I scare you, little Lena? I thought maybe you'd like somebody to walk you home."

She was so thankful she could have cried. She walked close against him, hanging on to the sleeve of his old duck coat. He had never been waiting for her like that before.

Papa said, "Did you all get along?"

"I don't know," she said carefully. It occurred to her

that, during a whole day of talking, Mrs. Chism hadn't asked what her name was. Papa took her satchel. With a sinking feeling she knew she was going to have to explain the book—and how could she, when she didn't even know what she had grabbed? "She wants me tomorrow."

"Then you either did a good job or she's desperate for company," Papa chuckled. "Did she talk you to death?"

"I brought home one of her books," Lena said, plunging in. For an awful second she had almost said, "She gave me a book," but she couldn't get the lie out.

"You mean she let you keep a book? Or just let you borrow one?"

She gulped. "I meant—I borrowed one."

"Did you now?" Papa's voice sounded different. "That was nice of her. What book?"

"I'm not sure." She hoped he would think Mrs. Chism had chosen one for her. "She has all these books in her attic and nobody reads them, so she—so I—" She was teetering on the edge. "I asked her if I could read one. I really did, Papa."

"And what did she say?"

"She said she might sell them someday, because they belonged to Mr. Chism—he's dead—and some belonged to her daughter that won't ever visit her." She snatched at all the distracting facts she could recall. "Because she lives in a saloon in Milwarker, with the butcher."

Papa laughed. "Milwaukee," he corrected. She held her breath, but that was all he said.

They walked along in the dark. Looking up at the trusting tilt of Papa's head against the sky, she thought of something that turned her hands to ice. Somehow, after she had read that terrible wonderful forbidden book, she had to get it back into the attic.

Five

LENA HAD GRABBED *Professor Gurshell's Illustrated Atlas of the World—Being a Compendium of Statistical, Descriptive, Chronological, Geographical, Astronomical and Political Information Respecting All the Peoples and Nations of the Earth.*

Claudie said, "My, he nearly wrote a book just naming it."

They all stood at the table as Lena turned pages under the lamplight. Roy's nose was close enough to be a bookmark. When she turned to a full-page engraving of mountains, Papa put his hand down on it to stop her from going on.

"Now that's what I want to see someday," he said softly. There was awe in his voice. "Look at that. The backbone of a whole country. The tallest things in the world—a thousand times higher than any building or tree." He lifted Roy up so he could look down on the page instead of smelling it. "Those shiny mountains. In the mornings they're all lighted up while it's still dark down where you are."

Lena asked, "Are they far away, Papa?"

"Less than three hundred miles, the closest ones. People here in town get on that old train, and next day there they are. I'd sure like that." He gave Roy a jiggle and set him down. "Anyway, if I don't get to see them, you all can see them for me."

Something in his voice, or her own tiredness, made Lena's throat close up. "You'll see them yourself, Papa, all the wonderful things."

"And it'll be just the same there as it is everywhere else," Claudie said. She went back to setting out supper. Potatoes. A loaf of bread. That bread, with the knife-slit still showing in its broken crust. She turned away sharply and went into the bedroom.

Papa gazed after her, his smile fading. "Read," he said kindly to Lena. He followed Claudie and closed the door.

Armilla was asleep when Lena set the lamp beside her own bed, but she let Roy crawl in beside her and watch as she turned through the rest of the book. She pored over the maps and charts and illustrations long after he had sagged off to sleep. The lamp chimney blackened. Outside in the weeds the crickets skirled slower and slower as the night chilled them, but she read on.

She was halfway to Mrs. Chism's the next morning before she woke up. Lulu was on the porch to meet her, looking like the dough for the ten dozen rolls Mrs. Chism had baked for the section hands. The morning went better than the day before. Mrs. Chism had left off her false bangs and had poked her own gray coil of hair full of hard-rubber hairpins. While Lena did dishes, Mrs. Chism described how she had stayed awake all night being mad at Tater's father for not bringing the boxes from the freight office after she'd told him to. She made syrup of her coffee with five spoons of sugar, and described the dinner she was going to give, and how many of her children lived close enough to come and how many didn't, and who else important she had invited from town.

By this time Lena was running the carpet sweeper and was missing most of the conversation. In a small room off the parlor she discovered a droopy yellow bird in a cage, and a great, carved, upright piano with little carpeted paddles underneath like an organ had, for pumping air.

"He looks sick. Don't he look sick?" Mrs. Chism asked, poking her finger at the birdcage. "Gooch knew all about birds, but I don't. I'm scared of the silly things." She made canary noises. The bird stood on the floor of the cage, propped by a wing, rocking. "Poor little Goochie bird," Mrs. Chism crooned, "you're sick."

"Mr. Kelsey might know about birds," Lena said. Besides the possibilities suggested by his name, Jaybird Kelsey ran the feed store and prescribed for animal ills as readily as the druggist did for people. "He sells chicks."

"I can't bear to see anything suffer," Mrs. Chism said, turning away abruptly. "I'm too tenderhearted. I can't even kill a chicken anymore. Right here—you missed some birdseed on the rug."

After lunch, high on a stepladder washing windows, Lena wondered what would happen if Papa brought the milk some morning and thanked Mrs. Chism for lending her the book so kindly. She gave a start that sent her pail of vinegar-water plummeting into the petunias.

Oh Papa, don't be polite to Miss Chism, whatever you do. Just yes-ma'am her, and no-ma'am her, and promise to fix her fences.

She remembered how odd Papa had looked when she told him Mrs. Chism wanted him to go over to her Hawk Hill place. He had looked at Claudie, and Claudie had said in a strange slow way, "Maybe you going to be too busy to go way over there." And Papa had answered, "I think maybe I will be."

That afternoon Mr. Starnes came out in his delivery wagon, and he and Lena carried the old furniture and used carpets and boxes of old clothes down from the attic. Lena was in a sweat for fear Mrs. Chism would pull out the wagon-sheeted bundle of books and instantly miss Professor Gurshell's masterwork. But Mrs. Chism was content to stand at the foot of the stairs, wearing her bangs and a new switch of curls, and yell instructions up to them.

That night Papa didn't come for her, and she ran home and ate fried yams and finished her book. At the last minute, falling off her chair with tiredness, she scrawled her lessons and tucked them and the book into her bag.

Mr. Doans gave her homework a long appraisal when she brought it by, next morning. She was in such a hurry to get away from him that she blundered headlong into Winslow Starnes at the corner of the schoolhouse. She bounced off in one direction and her satchel in another. When she untangled herself, she saw Winslow dusting off Professor Gurshell's atlas.

She reached for it, but Winslow jerked it back.

"Where'd you get this?" he asked.

She went cold. "It's mine. Let me have it." She grabbed again. He held it higher.

"Hey, hold on a minute." She saw that his face was not suspicious but interested. "That's the swellest book I ever saw. Is it a birthday present or something?"

"Yes," Lena said. "No. It's a—Miss Chism found it in her attic." She was going to kick him in the shins and get her book back, much as she hated to do it. "I have to go!" She would not say please, even to make him like her. Elsie Rawley wouldn't have to beg him. "Give it here before I break your leg."

"Now Lena—" Suddenly he laughed, stretching out of reach. She couldn't remember ever seeing him really laugh. Only grin. It changed his face. "Now, you don't want to do that," he said. "Can I read it when you're done? Ask Mrs. Chism if I can."

"No!" she exclaimed, horrified.

"Then I'll ask her—"

She caught the corner of the book and yanked it out of his hand. She clapped her eyes shut. If it were torn, she would never speak to Winslow Starnes as long as she lived. Maybe not to anyone.

She began to run, examining it. It seemed all right.

43

She slowed down, feeling foolish, because Winslow was not following. She glanced around, hoping no one was laughing at her for expecting Winslow to chase after her. He just stood against the schoolhouse wall, grinning.

She hated him. At the same moment she remembered the real, forgetful laugh that had changed his face, and the lilting way he had said her name. She was proud she had something he was jealous of. She wished she had dared to let him borrow it. But the risk was too great. If Mr. Starnes saw it and mentioned it to Mrs. Chism— she didn't want even to imagine it.

It was enough to worry what Papa or Claudie might innocently reveal, trying to show their appreciation. Lena sure did eat up that book you gave her. . . .

Surely they had more important things to think about. She had to believe they did, because she had already decided to take another book when she returned this one.

Mrs. Chism met her at the door holding the birdcage. Her hair hung down her back, long and girlish, and her face was crumpled with concern. The little bird fell over, struggled up on propped wings, and toppled again.

"It's worse than yesterday. I can't stand this. Can't you see it's suffering? What am I going to do?" Before Lena could open her mouth she rushed on, "You run and get Jaybird Kelsey—no, hell, he can't leave the store." She grabbed the tasseled cover she used on the cage and slipped it down over the bars. "Take it to Mr. Kelsey. Go straight there and ask him what to do."

Lena nodded. She wished it could be anybody else but Mr. Kelsey, after the way she had treated his bow-tie prize. She took the cage gently and started off.

"Wait," Mrs. Chism ordered. She braced herself. "If he thinks—if he says nothing can be done—tell him, would he be so kind . . ." She tried to think of a way to say it. "So kind as to put it out of its misery."

"I'll tell him," Lena murmured. She could feel the bird flailing and resting, flailing and resting inside the dark cage.

She walked as fast as she could without jouncing the cage too much. When it got heavy she changed hands and carried the satchel with the tired one. People glanced out of the first houses as she came to the edge of town. Mr. Kelsey's feed store was between the freight depot and the biggest saloon. He was loading a wagon for somebody when she hurried up. His shoulder was yellow with cottonseed dust.

"Well, Miss Lena," he said when she had explained, "let's have a look." He didn't seem to remember the contest at all. He lifted the cover and slowly opened the cage door. The little bird fluttered in an effort to stay upright and face the five-pointed thing easing toward it.

Mr. Kelsey brought it out and studied it inside his dusty hand. His lips pursed above his frizzled goatee, and he slowly shook his head. Lena followed him through the warm smell of feed as he went to the back of the store and put the bird into a small box. He handed the empty cage back to her.

"Can't you help him?" she asked. "Can't you make him well?"

"No, I can't, Miss Lena. That's a fact. You tell Mary Tom I'll keep it for her. Understand? Tell her I'll look around and try to find her another bird."

"She's scared of them," Lena said.

"What's that?"

"She might not want another one—she's scared of birds."

Mr. Kelsey laughed. "You don't say. Then tell her I have some Boston fern that would be a thing of beauty hanging out of that birdcage, if she'd care to bear up bravely and convert. Unless she's scared of fern, too."

Lena refused to return his smile. She was sad for the bird no one could help. It made her think of Bullet. He had been an old, stand-offish dog, wary of people by the time they had taken him in, but she loved him. Bitterness made her fingers curl into fists. She didn't want to know what happened to him any more than she wanted to imagine what Jaybird Kelsey would do when she left with the empty cage. Everything had to die, she knew that. But it hurt her when death came without the healing help of love and kind regret.

When she got back, Mrs. Chism was furiously beating a carpet she had flung over the clothesline. A pall of dust hung around her. She looked at the empty cage and kept on slapping, whap, whap, as if she were punishing the carpet for the little bird's death.

They washed the rest of the windows that morning. Mrs. Chism's sad face gazed from inside the house, her finger tapping the spots that Lena missed. Lena chugged up and down the ladder with her pail. From the top she was level with the little spiders sailing past on their gossamer threads. Wouldln't that be wonderful. Just to leap off the roof and fly through sunlight to a new place. Shiny mountains.

She had been so upset by the bird that she had dropped her satchel at the foot of the attic stairs with hardly a thought. Now, as Mrs. Chism started lunch, she seized the chance to carry it silently up the stairs into the attic. Walking on her toes—as if that would keep the floor from creaking—she turned back the wagon sheet and added the atlas to the pile of books. She drew out *Pearls from the American Poets* and slid it into her satchel. In the kitchen the clang of pots and pans stopped. (Girl—what are you doing up there?) In panic, she shoved the wagon sheet back, and scuttled down the steps. She dropped the bulging satchel where it had been and drew a calming breath. For somebody without much practice, she was getting to be expert at deception.

Halfway through their chicken and dumplings, Mrs. Chism pushed back her plate. "Do you think my little bird is in heaven?" she asked.

Lena choked and swallowed and took a gulp of buttermilk. It was sad, but it struck her as funny coming out of Mrs. Chism's mean old face.

Before she could catch herself, Lena said, to comfort her, "Are not five sparrows sold for two farthings, and not one of them is forgotten before God?" She ducked her head into her shoulders as Mrs. Chism stared at her.

"It says that?"

"Saint Luke," Lena said, to spread the blame a little. Couldn't she have said *anything* that didn't flaunt book learning?

"I'm glad," Mrs. Chism said. "Poor old Goochie bird." She studied her plate a moment, then drew it forward under her chins and finished eating.

That afternoon Lena got to see the bathroom. Even Claudie hadn't seen it, but she said she bet there was one, because Mrs. Chism disappeared occasionally into a little dark room made from what used to be two closets between bedrooms.

Lena went in to clean it, and stood gazing while her suds got cold. A grand, high-sided tub was enclosed in carved wood. It had a hole in its bottom to drain the water mysteriously away. Against the other wall was a privy seat, and above it, hanging like doom, was a water tank. All right there inside the house. It didn't seem natural. She was surprised that Mrs. Chism, being so finicky, would think an indoor privy was sanitary enough to want one.

Maybe it was mostly for show, because Lena had already cleaned the chamber pot Mrs. Chism kept under her bed. She fingered the slick roll of paper hanging beside the smooth, waxed seat. Just as she mustered the nerve to tear off a piece to show at home, she glimpsed someone leaning toward her.

She jumped a foot before she saw that the spiky plaits and rascal face were hers, staring from the biggest mirror she had ever seen. Her startled mouth twirled up in recognition, making cheeks with baby fat still in them. Her accomplice laughed and slid out of the mirror as Lena bent to tear off a strip of paper. She anchored it safely under her garter and got to work. It didn't occur to her to try the seat—there was still an outhouse beyond the back fence, as Mrs. Chism had pointed out the first time Lena began to look desperate.

When she had finished cleaning and come out, Mrs. Chism was yelling at someone from the back porch. Lena peeped through the kitchen window and saw

47

Henry Haney, Tater's father, standing in the yard, spraddle-legged from having just taken the wallop of one of Mrs. Chism's rebukes.

"What do you expect, when you're three days late?" she yelled at him. "Hell, I don't need you now. I already told Ben Sills to come this afternoon and bring those boxes from the freight office. You had your chance, Henry. I would have paid you what I'll pay him. But you didn't bother to show up and he *will*."

"I'm here now," Mr. Haney said. He had a mustache like Teddy Roosevelt's, but not so much face. He seemed to be hiding behind a small, worn scrub brush.

"But you're leaving," she said pointedly. She propped her hands where her hips used to be. "I've lost all the sleep over you I'm going to. I got a hand now that can work circles around you and that boy of yours, and he does what he says he'll do. So I'm warning you, you either shape up fast or move out.

She glared down at him from the top step. He stared straight back at her without moving. Under the brush his mouth made a thin, sun-cracked line. That level stare, exactly like Tater's, was meant as much for Papa as for Mrs. Chism. Together they were a threat he had to stare down, because silence was the only weapon he had against words.

Just as Lena thought her held breath would burst, he turned and walked out of the yard. At the back gate he spit his tobacco juice at the fencepost and got into his shabby wagon and jolted away.

"Go shut the gate," Mrs. Chism snapped. She was furious. Lena obeyed. They stood on the porch watching his raised dust drift away. "Damn that whole bunch—they're more trouble than they're worth."

Why did you have to single out Papa special, Lena wanted to ask. Lots of other people work for you, too. Why do you try to make Papa sound like your favorite? We don't want your favors.

"Something I meant to tell you." Leftover anger made Mrs. Chism's voice crisp. "The day I give my dinner and you're helping, I want you to say 'Yes ma'am' when you answer me or my guests, you hear?"

"All right," Lena said, perplexed.

Mrs. Chism propped her hands on her hips again, deliberately, and stared. It took Lena a minute to understand.

"Yes ma'am," she said.

Six

MIDAFTERNOON PAPA CAME with a wagonload of crates and barrels from the freight office. Mrs. Chism broke into cornmeal chuckles, rubbing her hands as if he had just delivered a twelve-course dinner.

"My order from the catalogue—finally," she cried. "My coat! And the piano rolls! And the gasoline stove— did you ever see a gasoline stove, Ben?"

"I heard about them, is all," Papa said. He gave Lena a wink as he rolled out a barrel of sugar and hustled it up onto the porch. She saw that he wouldn't have a chance to thank Mrs. Chism for lending her the book.

"I try to be the first one around here to keep up with all the latest things." Mrs. Chism sighed. It was a burden she bravely bore for the good of the town. "Hell, they didn't send me my galvanized roofing."

"It's there. I have to bring it with the next load," Papa said. He and Lena grinned secretly as they carried in another barrel marked DISHES.

"I like to get my Christmas shopping done early," Mrs. Chism said, not waiting for them to come back within earshot. "That way, I don't have to wait to start using what I get *me*." She milled a long laugh. Papa looked out the window at her, standing happy as a child at the tailgate of the wagon, and gently shook his head.

It was nearly night when Papa got the last load into the house and uncrated. Mrs. Chism looked up from her treasures long enough to tell Lena to go on home on the wagon.

"Wait," she called as they started off. "Ben, in a day or two you go out to the Haneys' and get the wire and posts and posthole digger I sent out there this spring. If the son-of-a-buck didn't sell it all already. I'm going to send you over to Hawk Hill."

Papa looked down at his hands. "Miss Chism, I sure would like to get all the cotton in before we get a rain. Could you send somebody else?"

"Hell, I'd rather lose some cotton than the sale on that place," Mrs. Chism said. "Since I sued that fellow west of me out there over the boundary, there's not any telling what he's done. Fence may be down all over. I can't have a prospective buyer seeing that."

"Miss Chism—" Papa had the same look in his eyes that Lena had seen when he and Claudie spoke about his being too busy to go. Was he really too busy? Scared? "You better not count on me. I can't go."

"Sure you can. Just check out the fence," she said. "Come back for some help if it's bad, but knowing you, I expect you can handle it all by yourself. It won't take but a day or two." She went in off the porch and shut the door.

Papa looked into Lena's apprehensive face. He made a soft laugh almost as mechanical as Mrs. Chism's. "That old lady don't take no for an answer, does she?" He gave Lena's knee a pat and clucked the team out into the road. "But don't worry—I'll talk to her again. She's got so many new geegaws to entertain herself with, she ought to be in a persuading mood."

"Don't you want to go to the Hawk Hill place?" Lena asked, struck by the words *don't worry* that he hadn't noticed he'd said.

"Oh, I don't mind riding fence," Papa said. "I just—

51

I just sure would miss all of you if I was way over there."

She peeked to see if his eyes matched the lightness in his voice, and he hadn't meant he was afraid of leaving them alone. He was staring at the black ears of the medicine hills pricked against the twilight.

"You're taking Mr. Haney's job," she said.

As if he hadn't heard, Papa shifted the reins from both hands to one. "Are you cold?" he asked, and laid his arm across her shoulders.

Claudie and the children were coming in from the field as they got home. Roy was pulling Brother and Armilla on a cotton sack, which was a good way to wear it out, but Papa just picked them all up and scrambled them around over his head and under his arms till they were squealing like pigs. While he did the chores, the rest of them shook up the fire to take the chill off the greens, and clattered plates on the table.

The minute Papa sat down, Lena laid *Pearls from the American Poets* beside him.

"Ah," he said, with a hunger that was not for food. He opened the heavy pages. "Look at that," he said softly. "My favorite of all poets. That loving man."

"Who, Papa?"

"Mr. Whitman." He began to read at random, careful of the words:

> *I see something of God each hour of the twenty-four,*
> *   and each moment then,*
> *In the faces of men and women I see God, and in my*
> *   own face in the glass,*
> *I find letters from God dropt in the street, and every*
> *   one is sign'd by God's name,*
> *And I leave them where they are, for I know that*
> *   wheresoe'er I go*
> *Others will punctually come for ever and ever.*

They were listening, barely chewing, when he stopped and looked around. Claudie said, "What did it mean?"

and they all laughed, even the little kids, peeping at Papa's face that the strange words had made strange. He turned a page.

> Failing to fetch me at first keep encouraged,
> Missing me one place search another,
> I stop somewhere waiting for you.

That night, shivering with fatigue, Lena filled half a tablet with poems she wanted to memorize. She was dazzled by Papa's loving man, Walt Whitman, whose poetry was like talking—or was his talking like poetry? And all those others she had never met. She would need to live to be a hundred, two hundred, to find them all and learn them all. There was such a space in her, like a rattling stomach that had never once been filled.

She was already copying again at the table when the others came in to start breakfast. She buttoned up the little kids with one hand as they came to her, and wrote with the other. Then Brother began to cry, and Papa brought him in, in a dry diaper, and set him in the crook of her arm. She laid her tablet on top of him and kept copying.

She was not sure what happened then. One moment Roy was setting the table around her book, and the next moment the tin pitcher of milk was toppling, and a white wave gushed over the pages. She screamed. So did Claudie, snatching off her apron to stanch the flood. Papa lifted the book and poured milk out of the center crease. They dabbed at it, bumping into each other. The red dye of the binding bloodied their hands.

The look on their faces scared a one-note wail out of Roy. Brother topped him with a screech of his own as Lena jumped up and tumbled him to the floor. She frantically blotted pages with her skirt.

Finally Papa took the book from her and set it on end on the table, riffling the pages so that they would dry without sticking together. "You're stupid!" Lena yelled at Roy. She grabbed him by the ear. Papa slapped her hand away. Roy raised his wail one note higher and ran to Claudie. Armilla, with a slice of bread in each hand, chewed and watched, fascinated. All at once Brother stopped crying and ate the crumbs she had dropped.

"We're all to blame," Papa said. "You should have moved it off the table for breakfast. I should have told you to."

Lena jerked the door open and ran to the end of the porch to cry. She sat by the kittens' tub, rocking, with her chin between her knees. The mama-cat looked out through a hole in the gunny sack someone had thrown over the tub for warmth.

Lena knew what "the vengeance of the Lord" meant.

Papa came out and stood behind her. He said, "I'll go with you to tell Miss Chism what happened."

"No-o-o," she howled.

"I'll help work for the price of it. She can't be too mad—it was a risk she took when she lent it."

Lena curled into a ball and covered the back of her head with her hands. Nothing protected her from his innocence, his trust, the hurt she would give him.

"I have to go by myself. Just me," she stuttered. "Please let me, Papa. Just me. I don't want you to go."

He sat down beside her on the edge of the porch. The mama-cat came out and walked across his knees. The kittens set up their thin faraway crying. Papa sighed. He knew. She knew he knew. She clamped her elbows to her ears and sobbed.

"You omitted to tell Miss Chism you took her books, didn't you? Oh, Lena."

She leaped up and ran around the house. She saw her feet flashing through tear-spangles, saw the ground turn white and slick where dishwater was thrown, saw the weeds of a fencerow loom up. She felt the prick of barbed wire. Suddenly she was calm. The worst had happened. The book was ruined. The happiness. Papa's voice reading the poem. His shiny mountains. Now there was only the dark tunnel of regret to grope back through.

She felt the wire quiver. Papa was leaning on the closest post. She couldn't face the disappointment in his eyes.

"I just wanted to read them," she said. "Books are to read. They'll just ruin up there. She don't care if the rats eat them—she's wasteful. She's ignorant and selfish."

"Calm down," Papa said from his post.

"You were as happy about the books as I was, Papa. What gave her the right to tell me no?"

"She happens to own them, Lena. They're hers to do with. Not yours."

"But owning things don't make it right! People owned slaves."

Papa saw that his palms were dyed red. He squatted and rubbed them with sand. His face was long and sad. "Still, you did something wrong, Lena. Do you understand that you did?"

"No!" she answered. She didn't understand. The only thing she was sorry for was making Papa sad.

"You robbed somebody."

"I didn't! I brought the first book back—I would have brought them all back."

"You robbed me," Papa said, rubbing his hands on his knees. "I trusted you. I would have stood up in court and sworn Miss Chism lent you books, because I knew you wouldn't take them otherwise. I want to trust you like that, Lena."

She held on to the jagged wire that stretched toward him. "I want you to trust me, Papa." She meant, could he love her, did he love her—or had she taken that from him, too? She turned away in despair. "I didn't lie to you."

"You led me to think a lie."

"I want so many things, Papa. So much."

"I know you do, baby girl. But you have to get them in a right way. I want things for you, too. For all of us. And sometimes I'm tempted. Lord knows I am. But we'll help each other hold out. All right?"

She moved toward him hesitantly along the fence. "All right." The sun rose out of a cloud bank, as lifegiving as his smile.

When they went in the book was drying on the cuptowel line behind the stove. She wouldn't look at it, but as she forced down her breakfast she could hear Claudie riffling the pages. Papa went out again, and came around with the wagon. He motioned her to get the book and climb up beside him.

When they got to the main road where Tater and Sammy had blocked the way that night, Papa turned the wrong direction to get to Mrs. Chism's. Lena didn't know whether to feel relieved or anxious. They were going toward the Haneys' house.

"Miss Chism wants the wire and posts they have," Papa reminded her. "We'll just go by and take them with us."

Now she knew to feel anxious. They were going to face both Mrs. Chism and the Haneys on the same trip.

She had only seen the Haneys' house from a distance. Up close it was ugly, set like theirs in a weedy yard worn bare in spots by the traffic of feet and wheels. At the side of the house was a brush arbor, and out of its top stuck a little whittled windmill, rolling in the breeze like a crazed sunflower.

"Look at that," Papa said. But he was looking at something else. "That well shouldn't be down-slope from the barn and privy that way—it'll get the seep. Miss Chism ought to be ashamed of herself, letting that go on."

They stopped in the yard. Three, then four children, stair-stepping down from Roy's size to less than Armilla's, watched them from behind a fence.

Someone in the arbor was using a grindstone, hidden by the propped branches of willow still shaggy with dry leaves. A woman's face appeared at the kitchen window, but a hand slowly let down a ragged curtain that blocked it off.

Then the grinding stopped, and Tater came out of the arbor holding a sickle. Lena felt her temples start to throb. He had on his father's hat, she guessed—his ears kept it from sliding down over his bone-thin face. He looked hungry. She thought of the bread with the knife stabbed in it. Why hadn't he eaten it?

Papa called from the wagon, "Is your daddy home?"

Tater must have had on his father's pants, too, held

up by galluses. He looked like the kangaroo with the pocket in Professor Gurshell's atlas. "He might be," he said in a voice as thin as he was. "Why?"

"I came to see him on some business," Papa said. He waited. Tater stared. The children edged through a broken place in the fence and stood behind him. Abruptly the door opened and Henry Haney came out onto the porch.

"What business?" he asked.

"Miss Chism wants me to pick up the wire and posts for the Hawk Hill place."

Mr. Haney spit expertly off the edge of the porch. "Well, I'll tell you—I'm planning to be using them posts and wire myself."

Papa said mildly, "Well, Mr. Haney, all I know is, she told me to get them, so that's what I'll have to do."

"Well, she must have told you wrong. Or more likely you just heard wrong. Because I done the Hawk Hill fences the last three years and mean to keep on." He glanced at Lena and away. Had he seen her at the window yesterday when Mrs. Chism was laying him out?

Papa drew a long breath. "Since we can't agree on this thing, why don't we go see Miss Chism? I'm on my way over now and you're welcome to ride."

Mr. Haney's chin suddenly jutted with pride. "I have my own mount," he said. "I don't have to ride with Sambos."

Lena took her breath silently and looked at Papa. His face was still mild. Untroubled, like a wall that an arrow had bounced off. Papa, stand up to him, she begged him in her mind. Smudge him right into the ground like Miss Chism did.

"Then maybe you'd like to go talk to her about it yourself," Papa said. "I can wait."

Mr. Haney looked uncertainly at Tater. The next oldest of the children came toward him. "Git!" he said. As his hand swiped out, the boy skittered out of range, blubbering a sound. His face looked like the kittens', mashed and unfinished. Lena had seen a face like that in Scattercreek. Feebleminded, Claudie had called it. She felt a surge of pity.

"You want to?" Tater asked.

Mr. Haney shifted his chaw and spit again. "Sure. I might as well go see her." He squinted up at Papa. "Since you got so much time."

Tater's face split in a grin. "Want me to saddle up?" Without waiting, he disappeared around the end of the barn. All of them gazed at the spot. He appeared again, chasing his father's horse along the fence. The horse minced and sidestepped out of sight with Tater at his heels, and finally they heard Tater stringing a row of oaths together as he tried to get the saddle on. Lena knew how he felt. He wanted so badly to show off in front of them.

Mr. Haney said, "What if I tell her somebody stole her blasted wire and posts?"

"She wouldn't like to hear that," Papa said. They sounded ordinary. Almost pleasant. One of those games where the winner is the one who doesn't move.

"What if I tell her you stole her stuff?"

Papa smiled. "*I* wouldn't like to hear that."

Tater brought the horse around at last, still skittish and holding back as if it had got what-for yanked out of it while they were out of sight. Mr. Haney took the reins and swiped Tater out of his way. He mounted in one easy, long-practiced movement, and unexpectedly he was different. He and the horse made a new kind of creature, with a power neither of them had alone. Lena could almost see how he had been in his cowboy days when fence mending was the thing he did best.

It seemed strange and sad that they couldn't all just be friends. It seemed like such a waste for everyone to be going set-faced in their own little directions. She wanted to say, Let's stop—let's just stop and look at each other a minute.

Then she knew why Papa was patient. He looked at everybody. He really stopped and looked, and saw inside.

Mr. Haney glanced at them, now that he was level with the wagon seat. "You better make yourself comfortable. I might be a while."

He rode off slowly. Tater grinned as his father passed

him, lifted the hat off the boy's head, and set it on his own.

Lena fidgeted. "Papa, he already knew he wasn't going to do the fences. Miss Chism told him," she whispered.

"People don't like to be pushed," Papa said softly.

Mr. Haney and the horse rocked together toward the main road. In the silence the gnats buzzed. Far, far off in the haze of morning, an out-of-practice band of wild geese paraded south, playing a song Lena heard with her feelings instead of her ears. Listen. Listen! Winter's coming. Changes. Hurry.

At the main road Mr. Haney paused and looked toward Mrs. Chism's, and rode off in the opposite direction.

 Seven

TATER GRINNED. The children's eyes slid to see what Papa would do. In the Haney's kitchen, a corner of the curtain lifted again.

"Well," Papa said patiently. He got down from the wagon and walked to the barn. Tater sprang to life and hurried after him.

"Hey! What you think you're doing!"

Papa opened the door of a built-on shed and looked in. "I'm seeing if you have Miss Chism's wire and posts."

"You can't do that," Tater protested. Lena stood up in the wagon, anxiously watching. "This ain't your place."

"It's Miss Chism's place," Papa said. "And I need to have some facts to tell her. I need to know I'm not being fooled again." He started to open one of the saggy barn doors.

Redness flashed into Tater's face. He threw himself against the door. "Listen, nigger, you stay out of our barn. My pap, he'll kill you as quick as he would a bug."

60

Lena sucked in her breath. Where had he put the sickle? He had had it and now he didn't.

Papa said mildly, "Now, Tater, I don't want to get you all into trouble. But if you don't let me look, I'm going to have to tell her you sold off all—"

He had started to open the door a crack. Tater suddenly seized the door edge with both hands and shoved it toward Papa. Lena shot out of the wagon and lit running. She saw the door crash against Papa and send him staggering backward.

She wasn't aware of what she had in her hand until her satchel crammed with *Pearls from the American Poets* caught Tater right in the kangaroo pocket. As he whoofed and bent over she swung again for his head. Papa's hand snatched the satchel and yanked it from her grasp.

"Lena! What are you doing?" He caught her flailing arms and pulled her close. "I'm not hurt, baby girl." He put out his hand to Tater. "Are you all right? She didn't think. She was scared you were trying to hurt me."

"Papa—he was!"

Tater backed off. His eyes blazed. "You lay a hand on me—" he gasped. "You lay a hand on me—" He kept backing. His face was a long radish, scalded with anger. "It's none of your business what we done with them posts."

"Papa, let's go," Lena begged, pulling him toward the wagon.

"I can't leave like this," Papa said, holding back.

Papa, she wondered, am I going to have to whack you in the stomach too, to knock sense into you?

"You can tell your old lady Chism!" Tater yelled. "You can tell her where she can put her barb'wire." He clambered up onto the porch. The woman was there in a cluster of children. She watched in silence, hoarding what energy she had, for growing babies. He shouldered past her into the house.

"Papa," Lena pleaded. She tugged him to the wagon.

He sighed, and climbed up. "I'm sorry," he said to the woman.

They turned out of the yard. The back of Lena's neck prickled, as if little hands were flicking up to ward off something about to happen behind her. A gun? Out the window? Would it happen if she turned around to look?

They turned toward Mrs. Chism's place. She breathed again. Now, in safeness, she wanted to cry. She batted the scared tears back. "Papa, he *was* trying to hurt you. He did."

Papa touched the welt on his cheek where the door had hit him. "Yes, but I forced him. I moved too fast. You don't back a watchdog into a corner and expect him to lick your hand. I should have tried to explain better. I forced him. I don't blame him—I would have done the same."

She crunched down inside her shoulders. "I guess I moved too fast, too?"

"A little bit," Papa said, and smiled. "Lena, my avenging angel. I was proud, you coming to my rescue like that. But baby girl, when are you going to master yourself?"

She crunched smaller. She saw now that she had embarrassed him, flying out to protect him from a boy brandishing a barn door. "I don't know," she said miserably. "Maybe never."

They rode in silence a while. "You will."

She shook her head. She could never be like Papa, forgetting herself as he forgot himself. It seemed that he stood at a distance, seeing that everything was very small inside immense space, seeing that events were blinks of time in endless time, not important enough to hurt him or scare him. She couldn't do it. She wished she could see past the outsides of things to the true, lasting part at the center that was good and exactly as it should be. Like Armilla's little face, asleep. Or Mr. Haney's cowboying in his youth.

Papa said, "At least we know now they sold off Miss Chism's fencing."

A picture flashed into Lena's mind of the Haneys toppling backward from the great explosion of Mrs. Chism's finding out. She almost smiled. "Will she make them leave, do you think?"

"I don't know. She's put up with their doings a long time. I think they'd miss each other, her and them—seems like they both thrive on contention. But she might, if she's willing to take the loss."

"What loss? I'd throw them off. Quick. If I had the say."

"Well," Papa said, blandly clicking up the team, "lucky you don't. You have to remember how it is, Lena. It's hard, sharecropping. Like running in a squirrel cage, knowing you can't stop. Each year you go into debt to keep your family alive, and while you're working the whole next year to pay back, it happens all over again. With us, we're different. We pay rent out of what we make, and if we can't, we move on—to a new place, new ways. We have some hope in our lives, enough to be a little proud and choosy. Folks like the Haneys, they can't leave. It's like a prison, and you get to feeling like you're guilty of something just because you can't ever come out ahead. And you itch to take revenge on somebody. Anybody. Because of the way you have to live."

"But Papa, it's still wrong for Tater to hit you and say what he did. And for Mr. Haney to ride off grinning and leaving us to wait. Why do you keep on trying to defend them?"

What she meant, but couldn't say, was that she could have used some defending, too, for what she had done.

"Nobody needs to be defended," Papa said. "Just understood."

They could see thin smoke rising through the tree-ruffles of Mrs. Chism's house. She was having mid-morning breakfast.

"I never told you, Lena," Papa said in a softer voice. "You would have had a brother, older than you, if he had lived. He would have been nearly Tater's age now. I think about him when I see Tater."

A big brother. She couldn't imagine it. Someone tall, to run to. "What was his name?"

"Your mother wanted him to be called Ben, too. And then there was another baby after him, born dead. Then you came, the year before your mother took sick—so now you're all I've got from that time."

She didn't know what to say. She knew he didn't expect her to fill the places of all those others he had lost, but she wanted to try, for his sake. She would have to find a way, as he had found a way to endure losing them.

"I'm sorry I hit Tater," she murmured. It seemed like something she could do for the brother she wished she had known. And the little baby. And her mother.

Papa put his hand on her knee. "I know you are." He handed her the reins and lifted her satchel up into the seat between them. Gingerly he lifted out the book. Or meant to. What came out was the cover, torn loose from the rest. Lena gulped. He reached in again and brought out a packet of pages trailing the threads that once held them to the rest of the book. Then another sheaf, crushed, and bits of shredded canvas from the spine. "I think Miss Chism's *Pearls* got pretty well scattered before the swine," he said.

At the look on Lena's face he began to chuckle. She couldn't believe it. He wasn't angry. The muscles of her stomach gradually unclinched.

"What a wallop!" Papa exclaimed in admiration. He pulled her close, startling a laugh of her own from her relaxing throat. "Now Tater's had a bellyful of the American poets." They both bent over with cramps of relieving laughter, letting their tension slack in whoops and cackles.

They turned into Mrs. Chism's yard, straightened their faces, smothered down the little snickers that flared up, and went around toward the back door where the explosion would take place.

As they passed the window of the little room off the parlor, Lena glanced up. Without the birdcage, it stared like a glazed eye. She thought in a rush, Not one sparrow shall fall, not even me. Her stomach bunched up again.

Out of the room came a jiggle of sound. As she turned on the wagon seat it became a song, joyful and sassy, the most captivating music she had ever heard in her whole life.

"Papa! Listen." The keys of the big carved piano must be flashing like a row of teeth with happiness. Papa began to smile too, and nod to the heartbeat pound of the rhythm. It was camp meeting shout and cakewalk and field hand chant, but put together in a different way. It was like two rows of bewitched dancers prancing along, each intent on its own pace, bumping into and caroming off one another delightedly.

Papa grinned at her entranced face. "Ragtime," he said. "Miss Chism got her piano rolls going."

They drew up by the porch and listened as the song tinkled to a close. Do it again! Lena entreated the silence. But Papa got down and knocked on the back door. He held out his hand. She got down with her satchel and stood beside him.

Mrs. Chism flung open the door. "So you decided to stroll on over, three hours late?" Her stare was a thumb fastening Lena to the porch floor. "I'm surprised you bothered at all."

Papa said, "Lena has something to tell you, Miss Chism."

Lena made a rattle of sound inside her dry-gourd mouth. She held out the satchel. "I took your books. Book. Two—one at a time. I ruined this one and I'll pay for it." She had the wild sensation that she was going to cry and laugh at the same time.

Mrs. Chism's grumpy face tilted into the bag. Her hairpins bristled like a scared cat. "Great balls of fire," she thundered, bringing out the pieces of book. She fixed Papa with a new stare. "If you didn't give her the thrashing she needed—I will. This was the most expensive book in my whole house. Now it's not worth a dime. I ought to turn you both over to the sheriff."

Papa said mildly, "We're both sorry it happened, Miss Chism. Lena was wrong to take it, even if it was just stacked away in the attic, and we're both willing to work out the price you would have got if you sold it. If you'll ask Mr. Starnes to set a value on it—"

Invisible smoke poured out of Mrs. Chism, a spurt of dragon breath. "You'll do better than that," she warned. She tried to think what. "Hell—I don't need a bagful of pages." She threw the satchel into Lena's grateful hands. "And I don't need you to work anymore either. Ben, you tell Claudie to get herself over here Saturday morning to help me get my dinner started. I have to have somebody I can depend on." Lena felt herself squashed again as Mrs. Chism turned back to her. "I can't have somebody stealing me out of house and home while I'm being as nice as can be, eating at the same table—"

Lulu came waddling out, ecstatic inside her rolls of fat at seeing Lena. Lena knelt and loved her up. Wisps of the old dog's hair drifted around them. Mrs. Chism backed off, snapping up her wrapper hem, exposing her shoeless feet in black lisle stockings.

"I'll tell Claudie," Papa said, looking politely away.

"Saturday all day for sure," Mrs. Chism said, put off her line of thought. "The dinner's Sunday and I've got two cakes to bake, and the ham—" Lena could feel the top of her head cooking under Mrs. Chism's gaze as she knelt. "With some good help I can get the pies and bean salad ready and I'm going to bake the turkey Saturday, too. Tell her I'm depending on her."

"She'll be here," Papa said.

"And Sunday to serve and clean up."

"Sunday too," Papa said.

The last of her anger melted. She patted down her sprung hairpins. "Come in here," she ordered. Papa followed her into the kitchen. She handed him something from a shelf. "I found this when I was cleaning out some drawers. You have a baby, don't you?"

"We sure do," Papa said. He was holding a little pin uncertainly in his fingers.

"It's a bib pin," Mrs. Chism snapped. "See? It says 'Baby Mine' on the front. Got no earthly use for it. Take it."

"Why, thank you," Papa said, as nicely as if it had been something of earthly use to *him*. He beckoned Lena in. "Look at this. Won't Brother be a daisy, wearing this?"

She was afraid to look at him for fear they both would burst out laughing. "Thank you, Miss Chism." It was for letting her have the book, but she was afraid if she told her she was going to stick all the pages back together and treasure it forever, Mrs. Chism would want it back.

"Hell, while you're here, get those castors polished." She slung her head toward some twirly, tarnished racks holding jars of salt and pepper and vinegar and mustard. "And the pickle castor. And the crumb set. Everything. Ben, I want you to come in here and see what you can do—my piano keeps jamming up."

She blasted off toward the parlor. The glassware chattered in her draft. Papa followed, dropping Baby Mine down the back of Lena's dress as he passed straight-faced and solemn. She gave a jerk and knocked all twelve spoons out of the silver spoon-holder.

As she wiggled and giggled all by herself the pin dropped into the leg of her drawers and she rescued it. While she was pinning it to the collar of her dress, the music started again. Lena began to polish, entranced. Her body surged to its glad beat. It had so many things in it. It strutted and tinkled like someone in fancy clothes, too proud to admit to loneliness. Somewhere behind its throbbing strength, a sadness hid: cities gray with cold, and people on trains, remembering home. Then up it surged again: ain't nobody going to put me down. Listen, this is my life beating, you hear it? This is me, saying things you never heard before. Move those feet. Accept it all. This is what happy is.

The piano stopped. She could hear Papa tapping on something. A sprinkle of notes. More tapping. Then the music again, tingling her toes. She bounced from cabinet to wash pan to drying cloth, dodging Lulu gazing up in adoration, and set piece after piece of silver to sparkle in the sun of the window.

What a marvelous invention—a piano that played by itself. What were they going to think of next? She remembered the first weeks in Bethel Springs when Papa had worked at Melodyland, cleaning up after the dance hall closed on Saturday nights so that it would be ready for church services the next morning. She had gone with him once, in the Sunday dawn, before the building burned, and he had let her softly press the keys of the piano there. Imagine people who could play that ragtime music, one hand tearing along out of beat with the other, splattering music all over.

She had to see what a piano roll was.

Lulu panted behind her as she eased to the door of the small room. It was ajar, and Mrs. Chism sat on the piano stool, pumping away like someone climbing through molasses in snowshoes. To her surprise, Papa was not working at the piano at all. He stood at the window looking out. The front of the piano was open and a scroll of paper, with little patterns of holes punched in it, was unwinding. The keys leaped up and down under invisible fingers. She gaped in fascination till the roll ended and its loose end flapped around and around. Mrs. Chism pushed a lever in front of the keyboard and began to pump again. The roll rewound itself. Mrs. Chism said to Papa's back, "Well?"

Papa turned around. "I couldn't say no to that, could I? We got ourselves a deal, and I thank you kindly. How long do you reckon it will take?"

"Oh, a day. Two. You be ready Monday." Mrs. Chism saw Lena over her shoulder. Her face closed up. "You mean you're done, so soon?"

Lena nodded, wondering if she dared ask to hear one more roll. But Papa guided her back to the kitchen, saying, "We better get the rest of that cotton out." He had the rapt look of someone about to burst with a secret.

At the first turn in the road that hid them she asked, "Be ready for what?"

"You adding eavesdropping to your list of crimes?" Papa countered. But he was smiling. "I sure would like to keep it for a surprise, but I guess you'd rather know it, so you can look forward."

"What!" she begged. "Papa, what?"

"Miss Chism's going to let you read her books. In fact she just might give them to you outright. I think she will."

For a minute she couldn't make a sound. Her mouth, like a third eye, grew round with wonder. "What happened? What did you say to her?"

"I just told her how much books mean to you. How hard you try in school. I even told her about the contest. And gradually she mellowed up, and she said she didn't see what good it would do you but all right, just so it didn't interfere with your work."

She sighed with happiness, staring off across the fields. She couldn't believe it. Mr. Cook's voyages, and Mr. Dickens and Mr. Alger and Mrs. Fanny Fern. All at once she got tangle-tongued with shyness. "I sure do thank you, Papa. That you took all the trouble. After I—" Disgraced you, was what she meant.

"I'm glad you're glad," he said in his warm soft voice.

Sitting beside him, beloved again, with her guilt acknowledged and bringing forth miracles, she let herself sink deep into happiness that was like warm goose down.

"Do you really think she'll let me keep them?"

"I really do. It's just going to take her a while to get used to the idea. She said she'd let me know."

"When?" she asked. Something had shifted into his voice. A little cold edge to his pride. Carefulness. She bolted upright to catch its meaning. "When?"

"When I get back from Hawk Hill."

"Oh, Papa—no." She stared in his fixed smile, trying to make it waver. "You said you weren't going."

"Well, I changed my mind."

"You mean she said you had to?"

"No. She said I didn't have to. But we both wanted something from each other, so we struck a bargain."

He was still smiling. She didn't know how to form the question. While he was gone—what might happen? Did they have anything to fear?

As if he had heard her ask it, he answered, "You'll be all right. I'll just be a few days. I'll just be over there behind the medicine hills, on the river." They gazed at the mounds, two little tan fists on the horizon, blue-veined with cedar trees.

"I wish you hadn't promised, just to get the books, Papa. I'm scared."

"Well, I think books are worth being scared for." He braced his shoulders, deciding to tell her something.

"I stay scared, watching you grow up with that good mind all hungry for learning and nothing to feed it with. I want you to know things and do things. Use your talents, pour yourself out. I want you to believe you can do anything you set out to, if it's good. Lord, there's so much ahead for you, so much you can be. The world's full of wonders and miracles, Lena. And I wanted those books for a beginning. I'd go further than Hawk Hill for that—I'd go around the world."

She stared ahead, struck gawky by his words. It had been so easy, when she was little, to grab him around the neck and paste juicy kisses on his face to say she loved him. But now, just when he opened up his heart and his grown-up world to her with so much love of his own, she couldn't do it. She didn't know why. Some kind of instinct, maybe, saying, If I went on loving you like that, I'd never leave, I'd never ache for anything else. Anyone else. She hoped he knew, in his grownness, what her feelings were.

In gratitude she said, "I'm sorry I can't work for Miss Chism anymore and help. But I'll take good care of the little kids while Claudie goes. And clean up at home, and get out to the cotton as much as I can."

"That's mighty fine," Papa said. "I don't have to go till Monday. She's got to get more wire and posts."

"Papa." She made a long tired sigh, wishing she could put her head on his knee like she used to, and go to sleep. "Will we ever get to work for ourselves? Why do we all have to work for somebody else? For her?"

He looked so surprised that she had the feeling she had asked something that had never occurred to him.

"What's wrong with working for people? That's what we're here for, to serve each other. The greatest people that ever lived served other people. Ministered to their needs—that's what 'minister' means. Even presidents, they're called the servants of the people. What do you think Jesus meant, washing his disciples' feet?"

"But Papa, that's way back in the Bible."

"Is it? Then maybe I better remind you of something. Those words you memorized—those words are not cotton, to see how much you can stuff in your sack and get rewarded for. They're rules to live by. They're to aspire to." She turned toward the unknown word. "You like that? It means to reach up to something high, with all your heart."

She gazed off, forming the word in her mouth. She wanted to aspire. But it sounded hard. As hard as serving.

Out of the corner of her eye she saw a speck against the sky. A bush? No, not with four legs. A horse and rider. Watching, perfectly still, not caring if it was seen. Expecting to be seen.

"Papa," she whispered, as though she might be heard half a mile away. "Look. It's Mr. Haney."

"I saw him," Papa said.

They moved on under his faraway gaze so like Tater's, until a line of brush hid him from view. She said tightly, "Papa, do you own a gun?"

"Something better," he said without a pause of surprise. "Got the shield and buckler of the Lord always with me. So do you. Remember that."

"Why can't he leave us alone?"

"He's leaving us alone."

"But he's not. He's watching us. He scares me."

"You scare you," Papa said. "He can't, if you don't let him."

She glimpsed Mr. Haney through a break in the bushes. Like the eye of an animal, checking, then closing, pretending not to watch.

Papa said, "Miss Chism is throwing them off her place. She said she's taking that wire and posts out of Henry Haney's hide, and then out they go."

Lena flooded with relief. "I'm glad. Oh, I'll be glad when they're gone."

"Now Lena, don't be glad for anybody's misfortunes."

She ducked her head. She had forgotten the tired woman, the dirty-faced children behind the fence. But his reproach was not enough to stop her from pouring out the fear curdled up inside. "Tater said his daddy would kill you quick as a bug."

"He did?" Papa asked. "I didn't hear that. But then

I don't pay much mind to mosquitoes buzzing." He gave her head a waggle with his hand, to shake the concern from her face. "Especially when that mosquito is about to get squashed by *Pearls from the American Poets*."

She knew what he wanted her to do. She made a laugh to match his. But out of the corner of her eye she looked through the brush again, and Henry Haney was gone.

Eight

MR. DOANS SWUNG AT THE FLIES that waltzed on his polished head in the honey-thick heat of near noon. He had begged the school board since September to buy a roll of the fancy screening that people were nailing across their windows, but it hadn't come. The flies buzzed off to the safety of the turnip on Sammy Haney's desk. Sammy stood in the corner behind Mr. Doans, nose to blackboard, repenting the expression he had used when Mrs. Doans told him to take his feet out of the aisle. She had gone to the back of the room to help the first-graders cut out paper pumpkins to stick on the window-panes for Halloween. Behind Mr. Doans's back, Sammy was gradually easing around. Finally he was leaning backward into the corner, scowling out at the rest of them, somehow looking victorious in his disgrace.

His scowl skipped Lena. Do you know what happened yesterday at your house? she wondered, trying to read his pointy little face.

Mr. Doans's droning voice stopped. He had asked a

question, and not a soul in the room had been listening. He yanked a round goldfish of a watch up out of his pocket, then cast it back. "Since all of you are more interested in the circus going on behind me than in the fall of Rome, you will stay in your seats for five minutes after the bell rings at noon." He marched off into the storeroom and shut the door.

There was a mass groan as everyone checked the re-action of everyone else. Then a shuffle. The short kids could either lean against the backs of their seats while their feet swung, or rest their feet on the floor without leaning against the seat backs. Lena let her feet swing, wiggling her toes to keep them awake with the rest of her, and tried to picture Rome crashing down. Mrs. Doans stepped up onto the raised platform at the front of the room, rang the hand bell and studied the watch that was pinned to her grand bosom. With a pert little glance toward the storeroom that said she was letting them out a minute early, she waved her magic ruler and released them.

They pounded out in a gust that rattled the windows. Sammy leaped from his corner toward his desk, strug-gling against their surge. When he got there his turnip was gone.

Glancing back from the door, Lena saw him droop with despair an instant. His eyes darted forlornly around, hunting rescue, or escape. But in the schoolyard the tallest boys were already throwing his lunch back and forth over the heads of the smaller ones in silent delight.

Sammy shot out into their midst, grabbing at the turnip sailing overhead just out of reach. The girls' gig-gles turned to squeals and suddenly everyone was laugh-ing and whistling as each pass missed his clawing hands by inches.

"Don't let him get it!" Elsie Rawley shrieked. She was so excited she didn't notice she was pulling Lena's arm.

Lena felt her throat fill with a screech to match Elsie's. She wanted to plunge frantically into their game—they were so sure of themselves, so contemptuous and happy.

Whirl that turnip by its tail just out of Sammy's reach. (Lena, you did good!) Who else had better reason to turn against him?

She clapped her hand to her mouth and stepped out of Elsie's grasp. She had seen his face. She couldn't laugh at Sammy Haney, standing up to his tormentors, his teeth bared like a possum's, his face and hair one furious shade of red.

Leave him alone. Just leave him alone.

She gulped a breath. All she had to do was say it. Shout it, a command that would freeze them all in a tableau, arms lifted, mouths hooting. Stop it—he's little and hungry. Give him his turnip!

She kept backing till she hit the schoolhouse wall. She couldn't say it. She wanted too much to be one of them. Accepted. She couldn't bear to think of their contempt turned on her.

And that made Sammy braver than she was. He dared to face them, his enemies.

She eased around the corner and got her lunch pail from the cloakroom shelf. She could hear them still milling and laughing. Sammy's voice spit out descriptions that would have earned him a lifetime of standing in the corner if Mrs. Doans had heard. Lena fled to the row of mulberry trees that separated the playground from the teacherage where Mrs. Doans had gone to fix lunch. Should she knock and tell her what was happening? Or let Mr. Doans come out of the storeroom when he was ready to handle it? It was his fault, anyway.

Miserably she climbed into the first tree, using the knotted rope someone long ago had tied high up in the branches.

The leaves were turning. They scratched together, dry and worn from a long summer of enduring. Along the limbs, the handhold places were slick, and the bark had been worn away by hundreds of shoes wedging year after year in the same crotches. She straddled a branch, tucking her skirt carefully around her black stockings, and opened her lunch pail. She stared down into it, not hungry.

Mr. Doans strode out of the schoolhouse. Everybody

scattered. In a second he was standing alone in the drifting dust. Sammy was pounding after a trio of big kids
who burst into the boys' privy and out again with smiles
of such satisfaction that he—and Lena watching—knew
what had happened to the turnip. Sammy whirled and
spurted out of sight behind the storeroom.

Slowly she pulled up the knotted rope. Other kids
were hunting spots to eat their lunches. To leave the
rope hanging down made it look like she was asking for
company. She didn't want anyone. Maybe she had,
other days. Not now.

When she had started school, the first person who
offered to be friends was a girl with a name like a song,
Faquita Garcia, but just as they had begun to know and
like each other, her folks moved back to south Texas
where the crops grew all winter. Lena had tried with
the others, but it wasn't the same.

From her perch she could see the trees around Mrs.
Chism's house, and the Haneys' beyond, but not the
field farther off where Papa and Claudie moved up and
down the rows while Roy watched over the little ones
at the cotton pile. I should be there picking, she thought.
How is the fall of Rome ever going to help them?

She looked down and saw Sammy pressed against the
tree trunk below her. Little slobbery gulps and sniffs
were making his shoulders jerk, and he was banging the
bark with a good-sized rock. They were the same hurt-
ing, bewildered sounds Roy had made when he tipped
the milk over Mrs. Chism's book. Only he had been
able to run into Claudie's safe arms.

She could see one skinny shoulder blade poking
through a split in his shirt. He would catch the dickens
when he got home. With hands that hardly seemed to
be hers, she tied the end of the climbing-rope to the bail
of her lunch bucket and let it down. She had so much—
a cheese sandwich and yams and a tomato—more than
she needed. She swung the pail until it touched his head.

Sammy jumped and dropped his rock. His fists flew
up in defense. He saw the rope and his startled eyes
followed it up to her. Without a moment's hesitation

he smashed her bucket against the tree and tore off across the field behind the teacherage.

For a few minutes she sat stunned, flooding with anger. She poked her tongue in his direction. Don't take it then. Starve and blow away. Who cares?

She pulled up her bucket and mashed it back into shape. The tomato had exploded. She put the sandwich back together and ate it.

As she started on the yams, the rope she had dropped wiggled and snapped taut. Winslow was climbing up. He hoisted himself onto the limb next to hers and grinned across at her. She grinned back shyly, hoping he hadn't seen what happened.

"What's that?" he asked. "Fried sweet potatoes?"

She nodded. Should she offer him a slice?

"With sugar sprinkled on top? I never tasted that kind." He wet his upper lip. "Sammy didn't know what he was passing up."

So he had been watching. She wondered if he had climbed up to tease her. Uncertainly she passed a slice of yam across to him. "You would've been mad at everybody too."

"You bet I would've." He pulled a fat ginger cookie out of his pocket and halved it with her.

They ate in silence, eyeing each other occasionally. Sammy had stopped running and sat against a fence post on the far edge of the field.

"Got any more books from Mrs. Chism?" Winslow asked.

"One." She searched his eyes. Was that why he was being friendly? "Poetry. But she's going to let me read them all when my papa gets back from fence mending." She hesitated. "And she might even give them to me. If she does—" She stopped. She didn't want a friend she had to bribe into liking her. But she had to know if he could be bribed. "You can read them too."

He looked pleased but not greedy. He said, "You like poetic stuff. I thought so."

She flushed hot, knowing he meant the Song of Solomon that had cost him the contest.

"I have a poetry book you ought to read," he said. "It's Shakespeare and all those fellows."

Her heart leaped. "Does it have Walt Whitman?"

"Who? Oh, 'When lilacs last in the door-yard bloom'd'? You like him? My father says he's vulgar."

"Oh no!" She almost fell out of the tree. "He's—kind. He won't break things up into what's polite to like and what isn't. He just pours his love out over it all." She stopped, embarrassed.

Winslow said, "I guess he's in the book. You want me to bring it?" She nodded eagerly. "You could keep it till you memorized all the good ones." He stumbled on, turning loose a compliment he had carried long enough. "You sure are a good memorizer."

The flush kept spreading along her arms, the way springtime sap must move through a tree. She expected to see little green leaves sprouting from her fingertips.

"So are you," she answered, remembering the way they had said those verses from St. John that had made people clap. She gazed out at Sammy, not quite willing to have so much happiness while he had so little.

"That dumb kid, is he still out there?" Winslow stared out, picking bark and letting it fall. His brow wrinkled. "It doesn't seem as funny now as it did while we were teasing him. I feel kind of stupid myself."

"So do I."

"You? You didn't do anything."

"That's the trouble," she said. "I just stood there. I didn't . . . anything."

He leaned back against a limb and looked at her. Suddenly he made that laugh that lit his face. 'You're a strange one, Lena. You know that?" He studied her, and his smile faded. Maybe leaf buds were opening in her hair. Maybe her mouth was unfolding into a flower. Maybe he had never watched anyone blooming in his warmth.

Out on the school ground, someone broke away from a group and disappeared around the building, holding something carefully the way a slice of cake is held. It was Elsie. With bait Winslow couldn't resist.

78

"She's looking for you," Lena said. She watched as Elsie appeared again, scanning the yard as she adjusted the fat stalks of her curls with her free hand. A chill passed over Lena. It was over. He would climb down. She fixed her face stiffly into an expression of indifference.

But Winslow slowly put a finger to his smiling mouth, and said, "Shh . . ."

Nine

IT WAS CHILLY when Lena and the little kids got to the field on Saturday morning. The white dew looked like ice on the weeds and cotton. Before long, on a clear night, frost would catch the whole green world asleep and take it by surprise.

Lena stuffed Armilla and the baby into the cotton piled at the edge of the field, scraping off the damp top layer first. Armilla heaped cotton around Brother until only his head showed. Roy would be their entertainer, guard and alarm system. From anywhere in the field, Lena could come running to pull a bee stinger or shake rocks out of Brother.

She slid the strap of her sack over her head and found the row where Papa or Claudie had stopped picking the night before. "You better be right there when I come to empty my sack," she called. "And don't yell for me just because you're lonesome."

"For snakes?" Roy asked.

"A snake's not going to walk up and bother you." He looked so little hopping up and down beside the pile that she relented. "All right. For snakes."

80

She started off, a hunchbacked princess dragging her sack behind her like a lopsided train. The sprung cotton burs snagged her fingers as she twitched the white fluff out of them and stuffed it into her sack. By the time she got really tired, the sack would be heavy and she could lean a little against its weight. Later she would tie up her skirt and strap on Claudie's kneepads, and walk down the rows on her knees to give her back a chance to straighten out.

It was fun working all by herself. Papa was already at the gin, and Claudie was over at Mrs. Chism's, finishing up the ironing so that she would be free to help get tomorrow's dinner started. Lena felt elated—so strong and happy she could pick forever. Two hundred pounds by noon. Watch their eyes pop when they saw how much.

A band of crows from the river trees crossed overhead, grating like rusty wheels. She laughed up at them, wishing she could remember how the ragtime went. Caw. Quawk. Caw caw ca-caw. She cakewalked a few steps, snapping her fingers. Caw!

At midmorning, when the sun was warm on her head, the train came into town from the east, whistling two longs, a short, a long, for the crossroads. Papa said a train could talk, if you knew its language.

She could imagine the bustle as it stopped, the people stepping down with fat valises, hurrying to meet other people waiting with smiles and reaching arms. And the mail sack lifted down, filled with words from everywhere, and the freight hauled off in the wagon while the locomotive leaked steam and the bell dinged—everything impatient to move on, to race the sun.

Then it pulled out and crossed the river on the long trestle, and gathered its strength for the slow, rising, westward pull. Into the lonesome grass. Space. Bleached blue sky and dried tan land, stretching and sliding finally to a city, a bustle of sounds and colors. While her body stayed in the cotton row her imagination sped west with the train, flitting beside it like its shadow on the cutbank.

Would she ever do all the things there were to do? Know enough? Have the courage? Be permitted to? Nobody she knew had. Papa came the closest. But even she had made a start. She had the strength of her longing. She had the promise of the books. And the promise of a friend. She smiled, remembering the mulberry tree and the smiling silence. She made a hairpin curve into the next row, dragging her cotton-sack caboose behind her.

At noon Claudie cut across the fields from Mrs. Chism's and came to nurse the baby. She made a throne in the cotton pile and leaned back with her eyes closed.

"That poor old lonesome lady. I swear she's going to drive me out of my head. You know what she had me doing?" Lena handed out the biscuits and bacon she had brought for lunch. "Washing the dishes *before* the dinner. Knives and forks, everything. All polished and laid out under a cloth for tomorrow. Did she invite the President?"

"I thought it was her children coming," Lena said around a bite.

"Oh, it is. Anyway she thinks they are, and some fancy people from town. But she don't get along with anybody. Who she think will want to? They'd have to be starving."

In a flash Lena saw the little bump of Sammy by the fence post as she and Winslow went into school, and the fence post standing alone as she came out to go home.

"If nobody comes, she can always drown herself in that tub of custard she had me making this morning." Claudie began to laugh, and Lena giggled, thinking of Mrs. Chism sinking slowly till only her nose and bangs stuck out. "Lord," Claudie said. "Two dozen eggs." She picked the cotton out of Brother's hair and suddenly hugged him up and jounced him till he cackled.

Lena filled a tin cup from the jug wrapped in damp gunnysacking, and passed it around to the little kids. Then Claudie. Then herself. She poured the last drops of water on the hem of her skirt and wiped her hot face. She had picked too fast and hard, and white fireworks were going off inside her pounding head.

Claudie said, "Miss Chism says your daddy's going to be gone awhile, mending fence."

Lena tried not to look surprised. Papa hadn't told Claudie. It seemed strange—she would have had to know soon.

"He told me he wouldn't," Claudie said. Her tired mouth turned down like Armilla's did when her feelings were hurt. She picked off the grass burs that had caught in her skirt.

Lena struggled to think of something to answer. He probably hadn't told her what happened at the Haneys', either. It felt odd, having a secret with Papa that Claudie didn't know.

"I wish he wouldn't!" Claudie exclaimed.

"Why?"

Claudie shot a quick glance at her anxious face. "I just wish he wouldn't, that's all." She got up and set Brother on a smooth spot of ground and gave him the tin cup to play with. "That old lady can make him do anything."

Lena bit her lip. Maybe he *was* doing it to please Mrs. Chism. And for the extra money it would bring, and maybe for other reasons she didn't know. But he was doing it for the books most of all. She couldn't decide what he would want her to say to Claudie about it. Maybe Claudie was trying to see if she knew what the reason was.

Being grown and deciding things like that all day was going to be hard. She watched Brother bang his cup and nearly wished she weren't going to be grown so soon.

She couldn't imagine ever being as old as Papa. Forty was—forever. Or even as old as Claudie, who was fifteen years younger. Nearer my age than his, Lena thought, glancing at her in wonder. In between us. Her face still so pretty, but sadder now than in Scattercreek with her people. Her hands cracked by the stove heat and the washing and field work.

All at once, she was sure that Claudie, in her mind, followed the trains the way she did. Only maybe eastward instead of westward, back toward the things she knew.

Armilla cried when Claudie started over the field to

Mrs. Chism's. Each time she tried to follow, Roy lugged her back, kicking and screaming. When Lena came to empty her sack, she brought Armilla a dead dragonfly, too beautifully blue to believe, but she was scared of it and kept on crying. When Lena checked again, she was asleep next to Brother with muddy tear tracks across her face.

Roy had dug a hole with the tin cup, and covered it with cotton stalks and grass.

"Walk this way, Lena," he coaxed, standing behind it. She walked forward and fell into his trap, slinging her arms and squealing in horror, but not so loud as to wake the others. Roy fell down with delight. "I tricked you! I tricked you. There was a hole under there."

She sat on the edge of it, his whole day's work, six inches deep, and emptied the gravel out of her shoe while her head swam in white lights.

"Can I help you pick, Lena?" he asked, falling upon her aching back from behind.

"No. You have to tend to things here."

"But why can't I ever pick? I wish I was you."

"No you don't," she said.

Late in the afternoon Papa came with somebody she didn't know in one of the high-sided gin wagons and loaded the cotton pile. Then he lifted them all up on top and they got a free ride home, gazing up at the clouds as they creaked along on a lumpy cloud of their own. She held Brother on her stomach, and almost slept. He was muddy on the bottom but it didn't matter. Claudie would be home and heating water for one of the greatest inventions ever: a bath.

The man stopped and let them out at the narrow wagon track that led up to the house, and he and Papa went on to the gin with their load. Lena carried Brother and Roy carried her rolled cotton sack and the jug, and Armilla carried the tin cup. Claudie was already baking cornbread to go with yesterday's pot of black-eyed peas from the garden, and Lena almost died just smelling the fragrance.

"You all start," Claudie said. "Then you can be cleaning up while your daddy eats."

While they were gobbling their supper she brought the oval tin bathtub in from the back porch and put it into the lean-to where Lena and the little ones slept. She poured a bucket of water into it.

When she could stop eating, Lena asked, "Did you get Miss Chism ready for her dinner?"

"Oh Lord," Claudie said. "I cleaned that famous bathroom."

"But I already cleaned the famous bathroom."

"But you didn't wash the soap," Claudie said.

"I didn't wash the—soap?" The spoon of pea juice that Lena was feeding Brother missed his mouth by two inches.

Claudie threw back her head in a laugh. "Somebody might of come in there tomorrow and found fingerprints or the Lord forbid even a hair on that pretty buttermilk soap from Paris, France—don't you know anything? You're supposed to wipe it with a wet cloth and put it right-side-up in the dish with the angel on it."

Lena laid her head on the table, too tired to laugh. Or maybe even to believe it. Claudie tickled her neck as she passed with a kettle of hot water to add to the cold in the tub.

Lena scrubbed Brother first, then added more hot water for Roy and Armilla. They were bathed and in their nightgowns, and still Papa hadn't come. She added a new kettle of hot water, shut the door and eased into the blissful warmth. Water covered her legs, but her toes stuck out, poking joyfully through the soap curds. She pulled the dripping washrag over her shoulders and closed her eyes.

Papa came home. She could hear the little ones being scooped up and all the voices weaving and then the quiet as they watched him eat. She could have lain like that forever, listening and resting, safe.

But the kettle was already boiling again. Papa would empty the tub and refill it in the kitchen. Claudie would get the next bath, then Papa because he was the dirtiest, not having spent the day washing soap. She got out and dried, and went into the kitchen in her nightgown to start the little ones off to bed.

Roy was telling about the hole and tricking Lena, and Papa was nodding. He met Lena's eyes and smiled. He was counting a pile of coins. A dirty strip of cloth was wrapped around his thumb. When he finished and handed the coins to Claudie, she said, "What's that for? We don't need any food—there'll be enough. With you being gone three days." She handed it back, to show him he had hurt her by not telling about the fence mending.

He got up slowly and put the money in the box on the shelf beside the mended *Pearls from the American Poets*. He motioned to Lena, and they took the tub to the back door and heaved the water out into the yard.

When they had set the tub down by the stove, Claudie said to Papa, "You be next so I can wrap that thumb up right. I'll just spit-bath in the morning."

"What happened?" Lena asked, suddenly anxious.

"Oh, I just sliced it a little." Papa waved his hand. "Not thinking what I was doing."

"Right through his thumbnail," Claudie said flatly.

Lena winced. "Does it hurt?"

"You better believe it hurts," Papa said. "But it'll heal. Good as new—maybe better."

"Can I see?" Roy asked.

"No," Claudie said.

"I don't never get to do one damn thing," Roy said bravely.

"Watch your mouth!" Claudie smacked his bottom and hauled him off to bed. He didn't cry. Always before, he had burst into easy little-boy tears. But not this time.

Papa sat down at the table and spread his hands. "I wish she wouldn't do that to him when it's me she's mad at." He glanced at Lena. "What did you tell her?"

"Same as you. Nothing."

She half expected him to swat her bottom like Claudie had Roy's, for being snippy. But he just said, so softly that it was almost to himself, "I put off things. Too long. Not wanting to worry people. I wouldn't have made a strong preacher. I guess the good Lord in his wisdom knew it, even though I wanted so bad to serve that way."

He got up and went out to draw a new bucket of water. Then another. Lena emptied the kettle into the tub and filled a new one. Then she found Armilla out on the porch by the kitchen tub and took her off to bed. Claudie was just coming out of the lean-to. She shut the door.

Lena crawled under her quilt and lay curled a long time until her back relaxed. She could hear the slow splashes of Papa's washrag and the clack of dishes that Claudie was putting away. But no voices. No little spurts of talk between them like other times.

Then Brother cried, and the dish noises stopped as Claudie went in to him. Lena drifted in the slow, soft, water sounds. Then they stopped too, and she dozed, but woke to the thin plaintive voice of the mama-cat she had forgotten to feed.

She pulled herself grudgingly out of bed and staggered into the kitchen where Bullet's pan waited, filled with scraps. The lamp was lighted in the bedroom, and she could see Claudie sitting up in bed, nursing the baby and reading the Bible at the same time because she would be missing church again the next morning. Papa got in beside her, but she kept on reading, half turned away because the Bible lay on the covers close to the lamp.

Lena backed off with the pan, trying not to watch.

Papa laid his hand on Claudie's knee. Claudie had wrapped his thumb in a fresh cloth and tied it with a little strip that went around his wrist to keep it from coming off. He leaned slowly and touched his lips to Brother's little head, and then to the soft skin where Claudie's gown was unbuttoned. Claudie closed the Bible and put Brother into his banana box at the side of the bed. When she turned back to Papa she was crying, and he reached his arms around her and held her tight.

Lena stuck the pan out the door, gave the mama-cat a pat, and skittered back to bed.

Ten

WHEN THE PREACHER SPOKE the next morning of the love that cast out fear, Lena nodded to herself. The love that healed hurts. And forgot itself. And gave itself away over and over. She cocked her eyes past Roy to Papa at the next desk, looking different with a tie and collar added to his shirt and his sleeves neatly buttoned. She would be married someday and she would know all that, like Papa and Claudie did. The idea scared her.

After the service had ended and the congregation had left, she took Papa up to the blackboard behind Mr. Doans's desk and showed him the stars she had got for spelling. He bent over, counting them, holding Brother in the crook of his arm and Armilla by the hand.

"The most of anybody," he said, smiling as Lena shrugged with pleasure. "You just have to be the best, don't you, Miss Magic Mind?" There was something sad behind his smile.

"Don't you want me to?"

"I want you to be the best you can be. Just so you remember that God don't judge you by the number of stars you get." Roy was slyly making a little row of squiggles along the bottom of the blackboard. Papa rubbed it out with his hand. He went to the edge of the platform where she had stood for the contest and looked out at the empty desks. "I want something for you, Lena. For all my children. And I hope I'm not wrong, because it's going to cost you pain, but I want it for you just the same. I want you not to know your place. You have a right to an education and hope and the chance to use your gifts. I pray to God you won't ever have to live your life by somebody else's rules."

The preacher came in as the last straggler drove away, and began to gather up the hymnbooks from the desks.

"Your wife's not sick, is she, Brother Sills? We missed her singing."

"She's helping Miss Chism today," Papa said. "For a dinner."

"Oh yes," the preacher nodded, "I think I heard mention." He beamed at Brother. "You're a fine, quiet young fellow. I noticed I put you to sleep." His eyes finally moved on to Lena. "Well now! You gave us a real show Saturday night." She flushed, thinking of the bow tie, even if he wasn't.

He and Papa gave each other little nods and Papa steered his family out into the sunshine.

They walked slowly down the road. Armilla was so hungry she began to cry, so Papa put her on his shoulders and she rode home holding on to his ears. They ate and cleaned the kitchen, and while Brother slept, Papa put Roy on a stool on the porch and cut his hair. Armilla took the still-blind kittens out of their tub and let them bumble across her lap.

Lena did her lessons. After the Fall of Rome came the Dark Ages. She wondered if she were imagining it right—a kind of wintertime swept by plagues and invaders. All that suffering: then, and thousands of years before in Egypt, in the Bible, and times after that. Soldiers cutting each other down, and prisoners rotting in darkness, and slaves used up like stove wood—all of them living by someone else's rules. Since mankind began, it seemed like, one group always banded against another group that lived or looked or thought differently. Putting the different ones down to make themselves seem higher. It seemed that by now, people could have grown enough to understand and like each other. Or at least to be moved by what they saw of themselves in everybody else.

Brother woke up hungry and was crying his head off when Claudie got home from Mrs. Chism's. The front of her shirtwaist was wet from waiting so long to feed him. She brought him out into the sun of the porch. "Deliver me from another day like this," she sighed, and kicked off her shoes.

Papa said, "You must have fed a lot of hungry folks."

"Who all came?" Lena asked.

"Mr. Jaybird Kelsey."

"Who else?"

"Nobody else," Claudie said.

They stared at her. She was too upset to be joking.

"Not one of her children," she said. "Not Mr. Gooch Chism's sister. Or the banker and his wife, or Mr. Starnes and his wife. Nobody but Mr. Kelsey. Just one person for all those tables set up and all that food. I felt so sorry for that crazy stupid old lady I didn't know what to do. She said go home. So I did."

In the silence, the kittens squeaked and Brother murmured in contentment, patting Claudie's face. Papa nodded gently, and swept the black snowfall of Roy's hair off the porch into the yard.

An idea struck Lena. "Papa," she ventured, "could I go up to Miss Chism's? To—borrow a book?"

Papa studied her face a moment. "And maybe cheer her up a little? Mr. Kelsey's likely doing that."

"He left when I did," Claudie said.

"I could pump the piano and let her listen to her piano rolls. Or something, maybe."

"Won't do any good," Claudie said.

Papa smiled. "Or any harm, either, I guess. You have a right to offer. Of course, Miss Chism has a right to say mind your own business."

"Then can I?"

He waved her off. "But I don't think any little ray

of sunshine like you is going to jolly her right out of that kind of humiliation by pumping ragtime. All right?"

She stepped off down the road, feeling a little too grown-up to wave back at them on the porch. There had to be something she could do or say to make Mrs. Chism feel better—and herself too. She didn't know why it was so important to redeem herself in Mrs. Chism's eyes after their trouble, but it was.

The house was hiding in tree shadows when she got there. Lulu was standing at the door, waiting patiently to get in. A big pink bow that had been tied around her neck had slipped under her chin.

Lena knocked. Silence. She knocked again. Silly old disappointed lady, in there with her piles of food and fresh-washed soap. She knocked again. Finally, she called, "Miss Chism, can I let Lulu in? She's waiting."

The door flew open so suddenly she jumped. Mrs. Chism, without her hair switches, glared down at her. Lulu squeezed in past the gores of her lavender taffeta dress. "Well?" She still had powder and paint on her face, and some of it had washed away around her eyes.

"I—I just happened to come by and thought I might get a book," Lena said, trying to sound more ordinary than usual.

Mrs. Chism stared at her as if she were Lulu and had just made a spot on the rug. "Out," she said. "Out. Out!"

"But, Miss Chism—" Lena said. She wasn't even in yet.

"A book!" Miss Chism exclaimed. "Can't you even wait for that daddy of yours to keep his promise and leave tomorrow? He could back out like everybody else does, and there I'd be, out another book and no fences mended."

"My papa don't back out on his word," Lena said. Now she was properly confused. "But I can wait for the book. I really—I really just came to . . ." How could she say it? Make you not so sad? Make you like me, while you're mad at everyone else? "I'm sorry about your dinner."

Mrs. Chism drew herself up a full fourth of an inch. "Just for your information, and contrary to the gossip Claudie's spreading, I had a very satisfactory dinner. Me and Mr. Kelsey feasted in real high style. If you don't believe it—"

She stepped aside and motioned Lena through the kitchen into the dining room. At one end of the long white table, still set with clean china, were two places littered with bones and crusts and dirty dishes. And between the two plates, in a pretty pot, was Jaybird Kelsey's gift of a Boston fern.

"I believe it," Lena said too heartily.

"You better." Mrs. Chism made such a ferocious laugh that the fern shook. "Big noisy dinners are a pain. Thirty, forty people, hell, who wants to go to that kind of trouble? They gobble it down and leave." She snatched up the dirty dishes and cracked them down on the kitchen cabinet. "Even Kelsey, that old goat, he hasn't eat this good in years. All my beautiful food. Couldn't wait to leave so he could start spreading around town how my very own children couldn't be bothered to come, or any of my friends. Damn, if he thinks I invited him because *he's* a friend, he's got another think coming. I owed him something because of the bird." She gestured angrily toward the fern. "And then he brought this thing, and I still owe him. I can't stand being beholden to anybody."

"It sure is pretty," Lena suggested.

"Hell, Gooch used to grow ferns ten times that big." She went into the dining room where her husband's portrait hung over the heavy, mirrored sideboard, and glared up at him. "You could do everything better, couldn't you, Gooch? Practically ran the whole town. People couldn't do enough for you. Your kids couldn't do enough. I couldn't do enough." Mr. Chism leaned attentively forward in his gold frame. "If you were here, they sure as hell wouldn't ignore me like I was dirt. But you're not here."

She picked up the fern and threw it accurately at Mr. Chism's head. The canvas split, and the picture crashed to the floor with the flying soil and crockery of the fern.

She dusted her hands calmly and turned to Lena. "Now you stop gawking and get home before I throw something at you."

Lena braced herself. "I—hate to leave when you seem so—" She wanted to say "hurt," or "lonely," but *crazy* seemed like the right word.

"The hell you do. You hate to leave without a bunch of these leftovers I've got. You think you can fool me?"

Lena's mouth fell open, and at the same instant she saw how desperately Mrs. Chism had wanted to be somebody—just like she did—and somehow couldn't be. Not to her children, or the town, or Mr. Kelsey, or even to Lena. She had to ruin her chances as sure as she stood there.

"I've got a surprise for you, greedy gut," Mrs. Chism said. "You're not getting one single handout. I'm going to eat it all, every last bite, if it takes me a month."

She stuck her arm out and strode the length of the table, bowling over glasses like tenpins. At the end she swept grandly toward her room. In the dim hall she tripped over Lulu, who yelped and skittered off in two directions.

"Damn, out of my way!" Mrs. Chism ordered the old deaf dog. She righted herself and peered around. "Lulu? Mama didn't mean to step on you. I couldn't see." Her voice dropped. "You love me, don't you, Lulu?" She noticed Lena at the end of the hall, and her voice shot back up to a yell. "Tell your daddy to be here in the morning—five sharp!" She disappeared behind a slammed door.

Lena stood uncertainly in the dining room. Lulu came up quivering, and Lena knelt and took off the pink bow, scratching and soothing her until they both stopped shaking.

Then she got out the dustpan and picked up the broken pot. She replanted the tattered fern in a big tin can from the kitchen and took up the scattered dirt with the carpet sweeper. She found the birdcage on the back porch and put the plant into it. She tiptoed into the little room where the piano was, and hung the fern in the window.

Something always comes to fill the empty space, she said to the Goochie bird's ghost, wherever it was.

Then she slid what was left of Mr. Chism behind the sideboard, and went home.

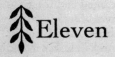# Eleven

IN THE COOL MURKY DAWN, Papa sat down on the edge of Lena's bed. "I'm off now, baby girl," he whispered. "I expect for you to be Claudie's right-hand man while I'm gone. All right?"

She batted herself awake, nodding. He had on his old oiled slicker that creaked when he moved, and he looked strange and big. Through the window she could see the team, already hitched to the wagon, standing in a drizzly fog.

"Now there's nothing to worry about," Papa said, giving her hair a scrub. "You'll do just fine. I might even get back tomorrow, late. But by Wednesday night for sure."

He turned to look at Roy and Armilla curled in the other bed. As he started off, Lena grabbed his hand. "I wish I could go with you, Papa." He stopped, patiently smiling and creaking. "I wish we could just ride and ride, all the way to the shiny mountains."

He bent abruptly and kissed her cheek. "We will someday."

He was gone so suddenly she wondered if she had dreamed him.

The unreality followed her all day. She carried her own little fog around in the big one.

When she got to school Mr. Doans had the new screens nailed over the windows. He stood in front of them with his chest out, daring the flies to test his handiwork.

While he was busy defying the insect world, a black, long-tailed rat bolted across the room and hid in a crevice behind a bookcase. The girls screamed and the boys crashed around, trying to figure how to force it out.

Mr. Doans held up his hand for order, and brought in his big slab of a cat from the porch. He knelt and poked it into the crevice to do its duty. The cat came unexpectedly face to face with the rat, and leaped straight up. It came down on Mr. Doans, scrambling madly, and broke right through the nearest new screen on its way to safety.

Turmoil again. The boys shoved the bookcase, toppling books out on Mr. Doans's clawed shoulders. Mrs. Doans shouted and knocked heads together, and Elsie threw herself into Winslow's arms for protection.

The rat shot out the other end of the bookcase. Lena saw it heading for her feet. Dreamlike, she stood motionless as it zipped over her shoes and along the wall, hunting an exit. For just the second it took, she blocked the path of the boys clamoring after it. As she was knocked aside, she saw it dart out the door and into the darkness under the steps.

And even better than that, she saw Winslow staring at her in admiration while Elsie clung unnoticed to his sleeve.

Mr. Doans shouted, "Lena, you deliberately let that vermin get away!" He tried to glare everywhere at once before anyone began to snicker at him, standing kneedeep in books. "Was it from your house, that you were so friendly with it?"

"Calmness, James," Mrs. Doans cautioned.

Lena gazed at him in astonishment. She was used to

hearing Roy yelling, "Armilla did it!" when he was caught in his own foolishness, but not a grown man she had admired.

"Great champion of the underdog you are," Mr. Doans muttered, rubbing an encyclopedia-sized knot on his head.

He finally blustered everyone under control. They sat down. Mrs. Doans scooped her first- and second-graders into a corner for vowels. Lena drifted off as their singsong voices made soft exclamations of surprise. Ah! Ooh! Eee! She was following Papa's wagon as it curved through the drizzle toward the two pricked ears of the medicine hills.

". . . the Insular Cases of nineteen aught one," Mr. Doans was saying. "Part of our colonial policy which enabled the United States to enact legislation for the government of backward people."

Elsie raised her hand delicately. "Teacher, is that what was meant by the White Man's Burden?"

Mr. Doans experimentally cleared his throat. "Since the Spanish-American War, the United States has taken eight million less-advanced people under its jurisdiction, in Cuba, Puerto Rico, Guam and the Phillipines. Yes, Elsie, throughout history the superior races have necessarily shouldered the burden of ruling the inferior ones."

A question lodged sideways in Lena's mind. She raised her hand uncertainly. "But what makes us a superior race?"

Mr. Doans looked at her a long time. Back in the corner the singsong voices trailed off as Mrs. Doans turned to stare too. Somebody giggled. Maybe she had said something funny.

"It is obvious from its achievements, Lena, that the Anglo-Saxon race is superior to any other."

She still didn't understand. "What's Anglo-Saxon?" She thought that meant English.

"Caucasian."

"What's that?" The giggles were growing.

"White," Mr. Doans said.

Elsie sat primly, holding back an angelic smile.

"Sir?" Winslow's voice rose out of the giggles. "How do you explain Jack Johnson? He's a Negro, and he's heavyweight boxing champion of the whole world."

"I couldn't attempt to explain why brute strength should be thought of as remarkable."

Winslow said steadily, "Booker T. Washington got an honorary degree from Harvard. Don't you admire that?"

"I admire the abilities passed down to him by his *white* father. And now, Winslow, we have digressed enough. Back to government."

Lena eased a glance over her shoulder. Winslow was smiling. A fixed, championship kind of smile. With a jolt she realized that the country had just fought another small war over the White Man's Burden. Her. She was not sure who had won, but she knew her friend from her foes now. Only who else was fighting? And which way?

With all her heart she wished she could leap out through the hole in the screen that the cat had made and run down the road after Papa's wagon. But she knew she couldn't catch up with it now. It was gone, like the trust she had felt for the people in that room.

Tuesday started strangely. Lena and Claudie were up in the dark to get Papa's chores done so that Lena could take the milk to Mrs. Chism before school. No one answered her knock, so she left it on the porch.

At noon she climbed the mulberry tree again. The day before, they had all eaten in the schoolhouse because of the drizzle, but she was sure that Winslow would come this time. Maybe even with the poetry book.

He didn't. She saw him standing for a moment at the corner of the building, looking at the tree with the kind of careful, indrawn look that Sammy had had.

He stayed after school to clean the blackboard. She waited until everyone had gone, to catch him alone before he started home. She wanted to thank him for standing up for her. Or for loving justice. Or for trying to flatten Mr. Doans and Elsie. Or whatever he had done.

But shyness seized her instead, and she said, "Have you learned any more new poems?"

He was startled. His eyes didn't quite meet hers. "Listen," he said awkwardly, "I can't lend you that book we were talking about." He shrank into himself, still scrubbing away with an eraser.

"Why?" She glanced around as he had, out of sympathy for him.

"My father said I couldn't."

"Oh." Embarrassment, like raw gusts of wind, came off him, chilling her heart.

"I'm not even supposed to talk to you anymore."

She was as embarrassed as he was. "Why?"

"I don't know. I think Mr. Doans talked to my father or something." He laid the eraser down. "I've got to get home."

She almost reached out her hand to stop him, but she held her fingers stiff at her sides.

Winslow said, "My father says if you all keep filling up the country out here, you'll have to go to your own schools." He began to erase again without noticing.

"Why?" Her mouth kept making that same word like a gate creaking.

"I don't know. Because you don't need to know the same things we do, I guess." He went on rubbing a spot on the blackboard that was already clean. Did he think he could take the color off? "He says you first ones, you're like a wedge—and the more that comes, the more trouble there'll be, and it would just be better if it all stopped right now."

His perplexed eyes looked off beyond her. What did he want? Did he believe all that, or was he just trying to believe because his father had said it? She was quivering inside, the way water skittered when a cold wind blew over it. Winslow laid down the eraser again. Quicker than he could move to leave first, she flung herself around and fled out the door.

Claudie was bringing in the washing she hadn't been able to dry the day before. While their own things were on the line, she had ironed Mrs. Chism's linen. She sent Lena up to Mrs. Chism's with it, running, so that she would be back before dark. Again no one answered her knock, but the milk was gone, so Lena left the bundle and ran home again.

When she pushed on the door it was locked. Inside, the baby was screaming. Roy opened a crack, then let her in. "Mama's looking for the cow," he said. "She said I left the gate open, but I didn't." Armilla was eating under the table, pushing her spilled gravy through the cracks in the floor.

"Did Claudie say for me to come help look?" Lena asked, in the silence formed by filling Brother's mouth with a biscuit.

"She said lock the door." Roy's worried eyes searched hers. "When is Papa coming back?"

"Tomorrow for sure," she said cheerfully. She had hoped so hard he could make it by tonight. She looked out across the field where the cow might have wandered, but night was falling too fast to see anything. She dropped the latch above the doorknob. "Well!" she said to their upturned faces. "We better eat quick before your mama gets back." She set them to racing and laughing while she stood at the window peering out into the dark.

She wondered what Papa was doing. Boiling his coffee over a campfire? Eating Claudie's bread? It was lonesome without him. Scary, a little. What if Claudie couldn't find the cow? No milk. And a debt to Mrs. Chism.

Papa. Fence fast and come home.

She lighted the lamp. If Roy hadn't opened the gate to the cow lot, who had?

She cleaned up after the little kids, too apprehensive to eat more than a biscuit herself. The wind gusting in under the house made goosebumps on her legs.

She squeezed out the door to feed the mama-cat. Impulsively she dragged the tub inside. The mama-cat followed briskly, checked the kittens, and cleaned up the last of Armilla's gravy with her sandpaper tongue. Her ordinariness was comforting.

Just as she bent to pick up Brother, Lena saw a flick of movement at the window. Claudie coming! She waited expectantly for the sound of footsteps on the porch.

There was no sound but the wind clicking gently in the shingles. The little kids dipped the kittens in and out of their tub.

Wouldn't Claudie call out, if she had found the cow and was going to milk her before coming in? Wouldn't she have to come in for the lantern and bucket?

Lena stood uncertainly in the middle of the kitchen, feeling prickles on the back of her neck. When she whirled around, she looked into a face peering in at the window. A sound stuck in her throat. Black hat framing a white face. Not Claudie.

She made her feet move backward to the table. Swooping she blew out the lamp. Now they were even—she and whoever was out there were both protected by the dark. In the instant that her eyes were adjusting, she saw the cloth-covered loaves of bread on the table, the knife handle. Papa there, calm. All weirdly long ago.

Roy said, "Leeena! What you doing?"

"Hush," she whispered. "Get Armilla and come stand next to me."

She felt them creep to her side. The kittens they had dropped on the floor went queek, queek. . . .

A fist pounded the door. Her heart nearly leaped through her ribs. She had forgotten to drop the latch when she brought the tub in. She wasn't used to locked doors. Lord, she begged, don't let them think to try turning that knob, till I can get there. She felt for Roy's arms, so she could slide Brother into them.

The fist again. A voice said, "Hey." A harder knock, that made them quail into a huddle. "Hey. Girl. I know you're in there."

Roy whispered, "Who's out there?"

Like a miracle her terror fell away. "Maybe somebody found the cow," she said calmly, the way Papa would have said it. She eased forward. She meant to drop that latch and talk through the door, just the same.

As she touched the door she felt the knob turning.

101

The door opened against her pushing hands. She threw her weight against it, but it moved her away, like a toppling tree she couldn't stop. She pressed the little kids behind her as she faced the shape that filled the doorway.

"Hey. Tell that daddy of yours to get out from under the bed and get out here."

The slurred words tripped something in her memory. Mr. Haney's voice. Pitched too high. Drunk. But Mr. Haney's.

"Where's he at?" The shape lurched.

"You stay back," she warned. Her mind darted— what could she grab to stop him with? I'm not about to tell you he's not home.

"He's going to pay for this." Mr. Haney collided with the doorjamb. His fingers scrabbled for a hold. "He done all this. She's taking my horse."

She? Horse? Did he mean the cow?

"High and mighty old cob. Whatever she wants she gets, and now it's my horse." His voice climbed upward into a shout. "Sambo Sills, get out here. I got something to settle with you!"

Another shape appeared behind Mr. Haney so suddenly that Lena gasped and swallowed a scream. Armilla let her little squeal fly out.

"Pap, get yourself home. You're puking drunk."

Tater. Lena cringed further with the little kids until she backed into the table.

Tater's arms caught Mr. Haney's and wrenched him around. "Did you swill that stuff till you drownded all your pride?" His ragged breath came louder than his father's as they struggled. "You're not going to blabber in front of niggers if I have to knock you down and stomp you."

Mr. Haney suddenly pitched off the porch, carrying Tater with him, and they cursed and fumbled in the dark and staggered up.

"Settle something—" Mr. Haney insisted.

"No! Not like this."

They wove off into the night, stumbling over each other as one balked and the other yanked.

Lena slammed the door and locked it. Roy and Armilla clung and stumbled behind her like the Haneys. "It's all right," she told them, making her voice calm. "Mr. Haney was drunk. He was just wandering around."

Roy put Brother on the floor, half reassured. "But Mama's out there. Will Tater take Mr. Haney home?"

She was shivering now that they were gone. "It sounded like he meant to." She strained to see into the darkness beyond the window. Trying to find Claudie out there would be foolish, she decided. She couldn't leave the little kids, and if they all went bumbling off in one direction, carrying Brother, Claudie could come home in another, and have to hunt for *them*.

"Where's Mama?" Armilla asked, still holding Lena's skirt.

"She's coming."

Roy said, "Is God taking care of Mama?"

"He sure is," Lena assured him, "and us too." And having a busy night of it.

"Where's Papa?" Armilla wanted to know.

A board creaked outside. Lena pressed her face to the window. A dark shape loomed beyond the porch. It broke apart. "It's your mama! She's tying up the cow."

They crowded out the door as Claudie started in. "Why you all in the dark?" she exclaimed, breathless and anxious.

"Mr. Haney came," Roy said.

"What?"

"He was just drunk. Tater took him off," Lena added quickly to calm her fears.

"You sure? What did he want?"

"To see Papa. He was mad about something." Unexpectedly his words made sense. "I think Miss Chism is taking his horse for the debt he owes her, and he says Papa's to blame."

"That trash." Claudie took down the lantern and a milk bucket. Lena heard her draw a determined breath. "I still got this crazy cow to milk. You all stay right here. But you watch the lantern. And if you see it go out, you lock this door and don't open it for anything. You hear me?"

"Not for anything—" Something in Claudie's voice shook Lena's calm. "Can we go with you to the barn?"

"No," Claudie said.

Why? Because somebody might rather they didn't get back to the safety of the house?

"But it was just Mr. Haney talking foolish." Lena's courage surged back. "Tater sounded embarrassed to death. You don't think—"

"You watch this lantern," Claudie ordered.

They crowded at the door while she listened warily and went out. The cow slung her head around as Claudie untied her, and plopped along after the lantern, her heavy udder swinging in and out of the light. At the barn the lantern's light dimmed to a glow the shape of the doorway. Lena stood on the porch watching, her head held rigid to catch the smallest sound.

A dog barked far away toward town. Watching someone's house. I wish you were here, Bullet. I miss you, old Bullet. Were you trying to protect our house for us, that night?

She hugged her cold hands under her armpits. It could have been Mr. Haney that night too, poking around while they were at the contest. Maybe mad at Tater for trying to get him out of their kitchen. Stabbing the table to scare Tater, not them. It seemed reasonable. Except for Bullet. Had they all at once got scared and hit him with something, to keep him from barking or trying to bite them?

It had to be something like that. She couldn't believe that the knife and Bullet had been warnings left by the Haneys, or a stranger, or someone they trusted as a friend. Warnings saying, We don't want you. Leave. Before this happens to you.

The glow of light moved. Claudie hurried from the barn with the milk. Lena locked the door behind her, and Claudie's face sagged with relief. She lit the lamp and turned off the lantern. All the shadows jumped into new shapes. It would have felt good to hide behind drawn curtains, if they had owned any. Close off the dark out there.

"Well," Claudie said, with only a flick of a glance at the window. "We can't stand here all night wondering if a booger's watching us." She made a for-the-children laugh. "We got things to do."

Lena came alive at the hint and gathered up the lost kittens. Old Nick, the strong one, had blundered himself clear across the room. Claudie put up the milk and went into the bedroom. She came back with a head-sized pumpkin.

"It was growing volunteer in the garden. I was saving it to make a jack-o'-lantern for Halloween, but tonight seems about right."

The kids immediately tried to climb up onto the table so that they could watch. Lena lifted them up. While Claudie fed the baby, Lena cut a lid in the pumpkin and scooped out the slick network of seeds.

Roy begged, "Make it big smiling, Lena."

"I'm going to make it mean," Lena said. "And put it in the window. And if anybody is still snooping around out there they'll see what I think about them." She forced the butcher knife through the tough orange hide. Squinting triangle eyes. Skull nose. Long snarl, full of jagged teeth. She found a candle and set it up inside the shell. When she lit it, and set the lid back, the face flickered alive. Monster. Breathing light. The kids said, Ohhh! together. They scrambled off the table and helped her set it in the window.

Claudie said, "Now we don't need the lamp, do we?" She blew it out. She and Lena sat at the table watching the two dark heads bobbing beside the glowing one. Softly she said, "A smart-aleck thing like that could make somebody mad, Lena."

It was like Claudie to think that. Patiently Lena said, "There's not anybody out there. It's just like last night. We went to bed and went to sleep like any night. It just seemed lonesome was all."

"Tonight they know your daddy's not here," Claudie said.

The pumpkin head stared into the sky for them. A seam of light escaped around the lid. Had people's lives poured out like that when they were scalped, she wondered. Back in Indian times? "I'm not scared of Mr. Haney. He's a big old bluster."

"You stay away from both them Haneys."

"But Tater made him go home."

Claudie leaned across the corner of the table, speaking under the little kids' giggles. "You stay away from Tater most of all. Hear me? He's the one has to prove himself."

"Prove what?"

"Whatever he needs to prove. How big. How much better. How much of a man."

"Not much of one," Lena said, to hide her anxiousness.

"That's the reason you stay out of his way." Lena jumped at the touch of Claudie's hand. "You had life good for so long, Lena. You know the world's full of loving people and kindness. That's a fine thing to know, and you been lucky, because most people don't see the world that way. But you just know the sunshine side."

Roy lifted the jack-o'-lantern's lid, and his own face took shape as he peered down into the skull flickering with fiery thoughts.

"When I was little, these men, these Whitecaps, come riding down through the flats where we lived, looking for somebody they wanted. They used to do that. Call a black man out on his porch in the night and just take him off. But this time nobody came out, so they began burning the houses. We had to run to the river bottoms, my family, because they burned ours. All we had."

"But that was back South, Claudie," Lena said uncertainly. "It's different here."

"It was there then. But it's like a blight. It's not someplace, then one day it is, and you know it's going to spread till it kills off what was growing so good."

She means like us coming here to Bethel Springs and beginning our new life, growing so good, Lena thought.

"Papa said we would miss all that, coming out here."

"We hoped you would," Claudie said softly. "Your daddy talked sad sometimes. About all the things he wanted to give you. That night after you said the verses at school, he was telling me. How maybe you didn't know how much he loved you, because he was always so busy and never did things with you, or talked with you. He said he wanted to do better."

Lena's throat closed up. She had wondered at the change in him since the contest, the ways he arranged to be with her. Making jokes. Pouring himself out like summer rain to help her grow. Because he loved her. She gathered the words tight, almost feeling his presence.

Armilla left the window and crawled into Claudie's lap. Claudie said, "You sure stretched this day out, didn't you, sugar babe?" She stood up holding her. As if she had felt the presence too, she added, "We all better get to bed. Papa be home tomorrow for sure."

Roy lagged after them, and Lena sat at the table alone. She tried to imagine Papa at the Hawk Hill place, rolled in his blanket by the ashes of a campfire, staring at the stars. Sending his thoughts out to touch them, and wishing them safe. Or at least brave.

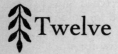 Twelve

WEDNESDAY DRAGGED ON FOREVER. All day Winslow stayed with a group and carefully refused to meet her gaze. Making the only hundred in arithmetic didn't take away the hurt. But what could she do? It was his problem, and he had to find his answer. But under the bitterness, she hurt a little bit for his struggle too.

Sammy wasn't in school. She couldn't help feeling relieved. Surely his absence meant the Haneys were moving out. She tried not to think of the tired-looking woman and all those children piled into a wagon with their pans and mattresses, hunting another roof for their heads. Instead, she focused her mind on the moment when she would burst into the kitchen after school and see Papa sitting at the table.

She ran all the way home. The dead face of the jack-o'-lantern snarled at her from the window. She stuck out her tongue. She didn't see the wagon, but it could be in the barn for safekeeping if some of Mrs. Chism's leftover posts or wire were still in it. She went in, holding her side. The kitchen was empty. Claudie must have taken the little kids to the field to try to get in the last of the cotton. No bedroll. No jug or slicker. Papa hadn't come home. The silence pounded in her ears.

He had said Wednesday for sure.

She went out onto the porch and gazed down the road as if longing could make him come into sight.

All at once she was running again, across the pasture toward the cotton. She could see the low pile, and Claudie moving along a row. Abruptly Lena veered off toward the Haney pasture that joined theirs. She had to know if they were leaving, or had already gone.

Her shadow, as long as a totem pole, buckled ahead of her as she scurried along the fencerow where the high weeds would block her from view. Finally she could see the gaunt house. Its windows glinted in the last sun like the pumpkin's face. The yard looked empty, but everyone could be inside.

With a gasp she crouched behind the fencerow sunflowers. Someone was coming toward the house from a field across the road. The black hat. Tater? She crawled through the sandpapery stalks and wiggled under the last strand of wire so that she could flatten herself in the roadside ditch as he passed.

Well, they hadn't left. But at least she knew what Tater was doing. He had a towsack of something bumpy over his shoulder, and a hoe. Grubbing potatoes? Anyway, not poking around other people's houses.

She could hear his feet crunching through a strip of field peas along the end of the corn rows. She mashed her nose into the ground as he climbed into the road and walked past her. His steps stopped. She had to raise her head and peer through the weeds. He had set the sack down and taken off his hat to wipe his dusty face. It wasn't Tater. It was Mr. Haney. Without his horse. Walking, just like anybody else.

She flattened herself again until she was sure he had gone into his own yard. Had Mrs. Chism really taken his horse to make up for the fencing he had sold? She scrambled through the bushes in the ditch, bent low until she was far enough away to stand and run. Now she knew where Mr. Haney was. But where was Tater?

Claudie was at the edge of the cotton, ready to go home, but scanning the fields all around. "Where you been?" she called when she saw Lena. "Did you have to stay after school?"

"I've been to see if the Haneys were still there." Lena huffed until her breath came back. "Papa didn't come."

Armilla peeped around Claudie's skirt. She had slept so many nights on her plaits that the fine hair had worked out of them. It caught the last light like a halo. "No. Not yet," Claudie said. Without Armilla there she would have said aloud what her face said silently: I'm scared. Maybe something's wrong.

"Where's Papa?" Armilla asked. Roy came over, lugging Brother.

"Coming," Lena said to their solemn faces. "Coming home." She gathered up Brother and the cotton sack he had slept on. The two stubby ears of the medicine hills stood against the cool twilight. What was wrong that he hadn't come yesterday or all this day, and night coming again?

Slowly they walked home. Claudie said tiredly, "Are they packing up yet, the Haneys?"

"I just saw Mr. Haney. I thought he was Tater, at first."

Claudie gave her a quick glance. "You didn't see Tater?"

"No, but . . ." She tried to think. In the barn doing chores? Eating supper? Off in a pasture, still and silent? Watching her.

"I don't like it," Claudie said. "I feel . . . strange."

"Do you think Papa had an accident?" Finally saying the words was like allowing it to be possible, but she had to ask.

"I keep trying to think he just had more work to finish than he expected, and he knows we won't worry."

"You sound like him," Lena said. The way he explained away the knife. The suspicions he had buried with Bullet, refusing to see evil.

Fear took hold of her like a claw, stopping her in her tracks. Tater was gone. The horse was gone. All this time that she and Claudie had worried about being alone in the house, about somebody bothering them—all this time it was Papa who was in danger. He was the one who did the dirty hard work that other men wouldn't do, and got their jobs. Papa was the threat that scared them.

"What is it?" Claudie asked, looking back.

Lena forced her feet to move. "Nothing." Her heart was thudding as if she had been running. She knew she couldn't rest until she was certain he was all right. "I'm going to find Papa," she said.

Claudie said, "Hush. You not doing any such thing." They went into the silent house and locked themselves up.

In the night Lena woke at every sound, and dozed and flung herself restlessly back and forth. Once she thought she heard Claudie crying. In the still, two o'clock turning point of the night, before the birds started or the sky came alive, she willed a distant clip, clip, clip sound to be the wagon. She brought it closer, closer—hooves, crunch of wheels, Papa coming. Even after she knew it was the mice under the roof, making a winter nest.

Lord, she asked, what do you want me to do? What Claudie says? Or what my feelings say?

What if I leave, and Claudie needs me?

What if Papa needs me?

Her body was rigid. Like those hypnotized people in pictures, with their heads resting on one chair and their feet resting on another, making bridges.

Between the medicine hills, and then along the river, he had said. How could she possibly find him, knowing only that? What good would she be to anybody, lost?

Just the same, she had to go.

Silently she rose and dressed. Her tough brown skirt, Claudie's passed-down canvas jacket because she was shivering. She held her breath as she carried her satchel to the kitchen and dropped biscuits and cheese into it. A jar of water. What else? She didn't know.

Lord, if you don't want me to go, let Claudie wake up and stop me.

She knew she couldn't go without leaving a note. But

she was afraid to light the lamp—for years Claudie had waked at the smallest baby-sound. She carried her tablet and pencil to the window and felt along the page as she wrote:

> Claudie I am sorry but I have to go find Papa. It is nearly morning. I will be all right. Give me a day and a night if I am not home then, tell Mrs. Chism to come find us.
>
> Love, Lena

She hoped she hadn't written all the words on top of each other in the dark. She propped the tablet against the lamp, and slowly so as not to make a sound she unlatched the door and tiptoed across the porch.

A wild burst of exhilaration sent her flying into the wagon track. Safe. No one could stop her now. Papa, I'm coming.

The cold weeds growing high between the ruts flapped at her legs, shedding dew almost as cold as frost. Her breath whoofed when the ground rose higher or sank lower than her feet expected.

At the turnout into the main road, she slowed to a walk and listened. No sound but the soft, gritty crunch of her steps. No movement. She steadied her breath. Left hand toward town. Right hand toward the medicine hills. She turned right.

Now that she was on her way, she felt calm. She knew she couldn't run. To make her strength last she would have to walk, steadily. Maybe all day.

She refused to think what she would do if, at the end of the day, she hadn't found Papa.

The road stretched ahead, a dim swath between weed rows. Somewhere in the dark it changed to sky. The air was like the taste of apples. She had never gone anywhere in the night before. Maybe that was lucky. She didn't know what to be scared of.

The same with Papa. She made her mind stop before she could picture him sick or hurt. She saw the team hitting a snag, a wagon wheel breaking—something so simple she would be embarrassed when Papa appeared, perfectly well and safe. He would be so provoked he might just take a switch to her legs. Oh, she hoped so. She would dance with joy.

When she looked back, the eastern sky was fading to gray. A weed rustled. She made a squeak of surprise as a jackrabbit leaped in front of her and zigzagged across the road.

Far off on the horizon she could see a dim light. Someone in a farmhouse was up early getting to the chores. Oh, Papa, be all right. So we can go back to the everyday happiness we had.

When the sun rose she was in country she had never been in before. The trees that marked the loop of river around Bethel Springs had disappeared. The farms and houses had given way to rangeland, emptiness, a frozen ocean of curly grass and scrub lifting and falling in rocky waves. She was the only boat, the only moving thing. The medicine hills had grown to haystack size, and the road struck straight between them.

She was walking slower already. Her cotton stockings kept wrinkling down into her shoes. She rolled them tight over her garters and marched on until they worked down again.

At midmorning she stopped and sat on the end of a little plank bridge over a dry gully. The sun was hot already. She ate a biscuit and drank an inch of her water. As she was putting the lid on the jar she saw a round cloud of dust moving along the road the way she had come. A wagon? It moved too fast. A car! Had Claudie sent Mrs. Chism flying after her to bring her home?

She shot off into the gully and crept under the bridge. Spiderwebs broke against her head, making the sound of hair being combed. Now she could hear the engine, a jangling roar, closer and closer. Was it slowing? She tried to squeeze herself invisible. Suddenly it thundered over her head, raining dirt through the bridge cracks, and passed on, clattering and fuming. She peeped cautiously over the planks. Two men in wide-brimmed hats. Not Mrs. Chism. If she had known, she might

113

have stopped them. She might be tearing along now toward Papa. It made her want to cry.

She marched on through their settling dust. The medicine hills crouched like giants, daring her to pass between them. She was close enough to see the cool dark cedars clumped among the rocks, and the hawks circling for their dinners. She thought of all the settlers and travelers who had moved across the flatness, holding those two points in sight like lighthouses shining through the desolation. All of them pushing west the way her folks had, foolhardy, brave, desperate enough or stubborn enough to die for what was out there.

The road lifted to pass between the hills. She was reeling with hunger and tiredness by the time it crested and sloped down again. The giants loomed, scowling through black cedar beards.

She threw herself panting on a flat rock.

The grasshoppers clacked away, frightened. Her weary mind probed their sound. Too hard? Too dry? She leaped up with a silent scream, grabbing her skirt close in a tiptoe caper that landed her in the road again. On the rock next to hers, a mass of sunning rattlesnakes writhed and warned, coiling over each other, darting small black words.

She stood tingling and gasping as they slid dreamlike into the crevice of their den. The blood boomed in her head. Somehow her satchel still clung to her arm. She headed downhill, dizzily scanning the road at every step for a dusty brown pattern, a small, jawed head. She shook and cried. Then she wiped her eyes on her hem and offered proper thanks that rattlers were gentlemen who gave fair warning. Still, they would have forgotten their manners if she had thrown herself down to rest four feet farther over in their midst. She would be dying now.

Dear Lord, don't let it be something like that, that happened to Papa.

She saw, off to the right, the trees of the river again. Somewhere soon the wagon had turned off through the grass. Monday's rain had passed this way. Wheel and hoof tracks were overlaid by the twin ribbons of the car's tires. She couldn't let herself miss those ruts leading off toward the river. In all that wilderness, nothing else could take her to Papa.

I will see you coming in a minute, she said to the silence. That little speck is the wagon. You'll stand up and wave your hat. And I'll run, run . . .

Papa used to say a prayer wasn't just a request you shot off to God like an arrow. It was also standing still and remembering you were a target. She stopped. They that wait upon the Lord shall renew their strength; they shall mount up with wings as eagles; they shall run, and not be weary—

But I have to hurry, she explained. Please. Help me.

She limped on. Without stopping she ate the last biscuit and cheese, and drank the final inch of water. The sun glared into her burning eyes.

Then she saw the tracks curving out of the road and off along a fence. Her heart leaped. She hurried along the ruts, wishing she could read signs like the Indians. It was clear even to her that the horseshoe loops led toward the river but not back toward home. Papa was still out there somewhere. The grass thinned in a damp spot and she could see the wheel tracks clearly, following the parallel hoofprints of the team.

Something else. Over beyond the ruts. The tracks of another horse.

A shiver passed through her body. She gathered her strength and began to run. Someone before her had been following Papa.

She crawled in under a gate that the wagon had passed through. This was the Hawk Hill place. She was inside Mrs. Chism's fence line. Off in a rocky draw, she saw cattle bunched around a salt lick. Somewhere along this stretching wire, Papa had worked and slept. She was so close. So far. And so scared.

She dropped down through a little empty watercourse. Tears sprang to her eyes. The rain had washed the soil out from under a post, and Papa had replaced it with a longer one. Its new-shredded cedar bark waved like a message he had left. She could see his footprints in the little extra pile of dirt his posthole digger had brought up.

How many miles could a fence go? To the river sprawling through the rangeland. Then along its bank maybe for miles before it turned again toward the road. And in all that enclosed land, no house, no moving thing but cattle. Birds. Wind.

Now, so close, she was afraid to hurry. Afraid not to. She had to know what had happened, and dreaded to know.

Only one horse, she was almost sure. Carefully following that fence. At night?

She had to stop running. Her head swam. Her feet clawed the dirt like two plowshares. She passed a spot where a strand of new wire had been neatly spliced into the old.

I find letters dropt from God in the street—

She was not going to be sick. She gritted her teeth and moved her legs. The fence posts swam and shifted. Sometimes she caught at the barbed wire and steadied herself.

What if he had gone home a different way?

Down there beyond the fence, the cottonwoods floated in their shadows. The thread of river glinted in its wide, sandy bed. The wagon tracks turned. She followed.

Up ahead was a windmill. A tank. The slatted wheel filtered light as it turned. She saw the team standing in sunglare. But she was dreaming. The wagon blurred and buckled. Cleared. It was real.

Her strange voice began to shout.

Silence changed to a rush of wind as she began to run. Churned ground where the cattle had come to drink. A campfire, dead. The bedroll in the wagon. Claudie's coffeepot against a wheel.

"Papa!"

The windmill creaked. She had to think, but she couldn't. She was numb.

"Papa!" The team jerked and snorted.

How long had they been standing there?

She climbed up into the wagon and turned a full circle, searching, close, far. Please, some kind of movement, a color. She went around again, straining, her hands cupping her eyes.

Down beside the river—something. She stared. Wind moved dryly over the grass and the mirror-leaves of the cottonwoods flashed messages. But something else—a blur.

Smoke.

She grabbed everything left scattered on the ground: maul, wire cutters, water jug. She had never driven a wagon by herself. But she could. She had never broken the law by cutting a fence, but she did. The strands zinged and whipped and parted for the wagon, and high on the seat, she urged the team down the hummocks toward that signal, that faint, blowing feather of life.

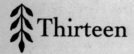 Thirteen

THE WAGON JOLTED down a drop-off and around a stand of willow scrub. Lena lost sight of the smoke against the sky, found it again, and headed for the tree nearest it, calling with a rasping crow voice.

The stem of smoke started from a sand spit. Roots of a fallen cottonwood reached up like a hand spread in terror. Someone sat against the bleached trunk. Someone else lay on the sand beside the smoldering fire.

"Papa!" The covered one lay still. The sitting one, as slowly as time, lifted his clocklike hands out to his sides.

He was smiling when she fell into his arms.

"Oh, Papa. I found you." He blurred in her tears.

If everything could just have stopped then, before she had to lean back, kneeling in the sand, and look at his ashen face, the mud crusting him. The grass clumps he had gathered to feed the fire. His muddy slicker spread over someone.

Papa reached slowly and took her shoulders. "I knew help was going to come somehow," he whispered. "But to be you. Lena. How wonderful."

A moan came from under the slicker. It moved.

She turned back an edge. Half of the face was Tater's. The other half was scraped out of shape. A cut ran through mud, across his eye and into his matted hair.

"Oh, Papa. What happened?"

"Horse bolted. His foot slipped through the stirrup—dragged him." He looked around uncertainly. "Down here. From the windmill."

"Is he—is it bad?"

"Broken leg, maybe. He hit his head, he's been out. Since—what day is it?"

"Thursday, Papa." She caught her breath, realizing that what she had thought was mud on him was dried blood. "Papa, you're not hurt, are you? That's Tater's blood on you—isn't it?"

He made that smile. "It's kind of a mixture, Lena." He put out his hand as her face contorted. "No, now don't cry, baby girl. Anybody who could come as far as you did is brave—"

"Papa!" Under his coat that crust had covered his shirt. "What did he do to you?"

"Well, he rode up to the fence on his daddy's horse, and fired a shot that scared us all—him, me—the horse shied off like a hornet. Snagged him through all that brush—"

She almost screamed, "Did he shoot you, Papa!"

He took her frantic hands and held them still. "Well, it turned out he's a better shot than he is a rider, baby girl." His eyes forced her to hold steady until she saw in his face what he had to tell her. "Much better."

She yanked her hands free, so that the truth could not pass between them. Oh dear God, oh dear God. Tater's arm thrashed out beside her. She cringed as she had from the snakes. "No," she cried. "No no no no—"

Papa caught her arm. "Hush, Lena. We don't have time for that."

She pulled free and would not listen. It was not real, it was not happening. Her eyes clinched shut. Her mouth opened and made a long raw sound to drown his words.

Pictures flashed behind her eyelids: Papa standing up

from the fire to see who approached, horse bolting at the blast, Tater scraped out of the saddle by tree limbs as if the hand of God had struck him in abomination. Through the brush, hanging by one foot, his head banging the ground. Why didn't you die? Papa moving, following to help him. How? Crawling?

"I got to get you home, Papa. Into the wagon."

"Tater first."

"Papa! He tried to kill you. I can't touch him. Papa— I can't. We'll send somebody for him."

"Good Lord already sent somebody." Papa leaned his head against the tree trunk, resting, finding strength for words, the smile. "Heard him yelling, way off. Got to him, finally, but the horse kept spooking. Pulled him loose. That was yesterday, I think. I was ready to start home."

"Papa, why didn't you just get into the wagon and *leave!*"

He looked surprised. It had never occurred to him. He said, "I tried to drag him on the slicker, but I kept passing out. Haven't been much help to him. Just keeping the blowflies off." He stretched his hand for her. "Lena. I hope I'm not dreaming you."

She clamped back tears. "Papa. Listen to me. We have to go home."

"I had so much I wanted to tell you. All the things I thought we'd have time for, later." He bit down on the pain with animal teeth, then his face drained back to calmness. "Couldn't remember to live every day like it was the last one."

"It's not the last one—it's not!" she insisted. "But we have to get back to town and get you fixed up."

He put his arm gently around her shoulders. She felt the gritty solidness of his chest against her face. "I can't be fixed up, baby girl. Inside—"

"Yes you can!"

"No. I can't. But Tater can. So I want you to get him back to his folks." He held her as her body stiffened and broke into helpless tremors. No. Impossible. Her head slashed back and forth against him.

"I won't do it."

"For my sake," he said patiently. "Don't grieve, now, Lena. This is wonderful, that we're getting to say last things to each other. Most people don't get to, or can't. It's what I held out for. So I could tell you how much I love you. And Claudie. And the babies. And thank you. For all you've given me."

A great weariness pressed her into submission. "Why was it you and not him, Papa? Where was the shield and buckler of the Lord?"

"I don't know, Lena. I wrestled all night with that, and you'll have to wrestle too, till you get an answer. There's an answer."

Her insides bled with his. "Oh, Papa. I don't want to live if you can't."

"I know. At first it seems that way. But if you live, then I live too, you see. Right there with you."

She held to his shoulder, for turning loose would mean dropping into a darkness she could never climb out of.

Behind her, a moan slowly unraveled. Tater thrashed and rocked. She blocked the sound. Every emotion. No.

"Bring the wagon closer," Papa said. "I'll try to help you get him in."

"You in first." She could feel his strength sliding away. What was left had to be for himself. "I can manage him—I know what to do, by myself. You first."

"All right," he said.

She leaped up. "I'll lay out the bedroll."

"For him," Papa said. "I would like—grass."

"Grass!" It was more than she could bear. She began to snatch up armloads, frantic to serve him and be on their way to help. Carefully she brought the wagon around until the back wheel was within his reach.

He gathered his strength. With her help he got to his knees, his hands fumbling along the spokes. He lifted himself up, breathing raggedly, and crumpled into the back of the wagon. Lena crawled up beside him and helped him ease all the way in and sag into the grass pile.

"Horse pretty close," Papa said in his whispery voice. "I could hear him last night. Find him, while I rest a little while." He turned his head and clamped down on the pain again. She knew he didn't want her to watch him that way. Heavy with misgiving she stood up and peered across the brush and river sand.

Finally she saw a movement in the distance. Ancient, strange shape, a head dabbing down and up again. Prehistoric creature, part of her nightmare. I want to wake up, Lord. Please.

She knelt again. Papa's eyes were closed, but his thin breath rasped steadily. "Papa. Do I have to leave you?"

"Yes . . . better to."

"I can't."

He opened his eyes. "Can't?" he said tenderly. "Remember. After this, you can do anything."

Smiling, he gave her a little push.

She got down, blind with tears, and stumbled through the brush toward the horse. Hurrying, because Papa wanted her to hurry. Why? Fear filled her mouth with the taste of pennies. She knew why. Her body tensed to turn and face the unfaceable thing he was trying to spare her. But her legs folded like broken sticks and she pitched to her knees clutching grass and praying incoherently. Help me do this—I can't.

When she stood up, the horse was moving off. She gathered her strength in an aching breath and jogged heavily after him into the next clearing. The saddle had slipped, and he kept sidestepping, walling his eyes to see what followed him.

She moved closer, numbed to a kind of calmness. When she finally reached out to him, he spooked again, and then stood shivering, blowing his breath suspiciously, but ready to submit to what had to be. A cut on his shank had a rim of flies. She gathered the reins cautiously, murmuring, smearing her tears away so she could see. By pulling on the stirrup, she got the saddle almost straight, and tightened the cinch. Mr. Haney's fancy lariat was dragging. She wound it up again and looped it over the saddle horn.

They went back through the brush. She understood why Papa had sent her away. This part was between him and the Lord. They didn't need her. She walked forward in her shell of numbness, parting the silence that surged around her. She could taste the pennies. At the fallen tree, she tied the horse to one of the finger roots.

The final shred of smoke from the untended fire rose up through the branches, silver in the low sunlight. Lingering. Leaving.

She said, "Forgive me, Papa. I couldn't say last things."

She went to the end of the wagon, into a silence where her heart pounded. He had coughed up blood at the last. She wet the hem of her skirt from the jug and wiped his face, and laid the green grass over it. The dirty bandage on his thumb was trailing loose. She took it off. The cut had started to heal—all the life-loving power in him had been trustfully making him as good as new. Her numbness broke, and she threw back her head in one long final wail of grief.

Tater slid the slicker down and looked at her with the good side of his face. She gazed back at him from the wagon bed, in an icy stillness. He was conscious. His hand groped feebly at his head.

"Godsake, help me," he said.

She gazed down. She had the power to drive away and leave him, never looking back. The right to. A life for a life.

She would say, How could I help him? I never saw him.

His hand fumbled, long-fingered, delicate. Not a farmer's hand. She thought of the little windmill at the corner of the Haneys' brush arbor that he must have made.

"Somebody!" he begged.

She sat frozen like a leaf in a winter puddle, watching his fingers probe his scraped face. The flies patiently moved away and resettled. She knew what they did. Laid their eggs under broken skin, and maggots hatched out, white, squirming. Her stomach tipped over. She held to the wagon until she stopped reeling.

"Girl, help me."

Every nerve and muscle said, I can't. I won't.

For my sake, Papa had urged her. She looked back at him in the grass, the sunken, long, familiar house of her father that he had moved out of. On his way to something better, another Bethel Springs. The hallowed spot.

"I can't," she said.

She knew, with a heavy sinking, how Papa would answer, whom he would quote. Love your enemies and do good to those who hate you. Give to him that asketh thee.

The words that had been so beautiful to say, so easy, turned to stone. No one had told her, not Papa, not the preacher, that they could change like that when they had to be lived, and crush her with their weight.

I have to hurt him back, Papa.

She got out of the wagon and looked down at Tater. His good eye focused on her. The other was sealed shut with blood. Tooth for a tooth. Mysteries. Wonders. How horrible to be lying there afraid you were dying in your sins.

Papa, why couldn't you give up on him? she implored. Why couldn't you—so I could too?

She could feel him waiting, certain and tranquil, to take up his home in her when she decided.

Tater raised his hand and scraped the flies away. Give to him? Love him? How could she love him?

She brought the horse over and tied the reins to the end gate. Carefully she unhooked the lariat and heaved it over a cottonwood limb. Wrong place. She pulled it down and threw again. Better. She made sure the end was secure on the saddle horn. Then she knelt by Tater, sliding open the loop at the other end.

His good eye followed it. "No," his voice rasped. "No—no!" He tried to raise himself on his elbows. It was what she wanted. She slid the noose over his head and shoulders, working and tugging, fighting his hands, until she had it under his arms.

"Don't pass out on me," she ordered.

She hiked up her skirt and got onto the horse. Slowly she eased him off, both of them trembling, until the rope came taut.

Tater grabbed it as he was lifted up. His knees buckled

and dragged. Heavily, his body swung toward the end of the wagon. He caught it, missed, grabbed again, and pitched himself toward it. Lena turned the horse back, and the rope slackened. Tater tumbled face-down into the wagon bed, crying out with gratitude and pain.

She looked down on him. She couldn't love him. But she loved someone who knew how to love him, and that was a beginning.

She brought Papa's slicker to put over him. He had passed out again. She laid the bedroll beside him and toppled him over onto it. New blood ran from his nose.

Stonily, she wrestled the saddle off the horse and into the wagon. Poured sand over the fire. Over their blood-stains. The strong weeds of another summer would hide it all.

At the windmill the team pulled over to drink at the tank, in spite of her tugging. She sat staring at the fence she had cut. Mrs. Chism would send Mr. Haney to fix it after all, she thought. Finally she coaxed the team along the fencerow toward the road.

They reached it in the dark, and passed through the gate. The jolting smoothed away. The team knew. The horse hitched to the tailgate answered something they said.

Lena turned up the collar of Claudie's jacket. She buttoned it tight, to make one more layer of numbness over the icy core of her heart.

In the night, the wild geese flew over, hunting the river. A jostle of voices, hoarse, urging. So tired. Exhorting each other: You can do it. Circling. Lost.

She dozed, and righted herself, and dozed. Tater was talking. "Hellfire . . . Mama save me oh godsake it hurts." He would start up on his elbows and fall back. Finally she stopped the wagon and crawled back and held his thin hand until he sagged off again.

A little chip of moon. If it looked like the letter C it was waning, Papa had taught her. If it looked like the front of a D it was cresting. Waning tonight. Toward the dark of the moon. Frosts. Seasons. What else could you have taught me, that I'll have to learn now by myself?

She looked for the Big Dipper. The Drinking Gourd that had guided her people running for freedom out of the sweaty Southern nights.

All those tears.

She could almost remember, from that night of reading, the words of Papa's loving man that she had stolen for her tablet—how had they gone?

I hear you whispering there O stars of heaven,
O sun—O grass of graves—O perpetual transfers and
*   promotions,*
If you do not say any thing how can I say any thing?

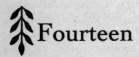# Fourteen

IN THE NIGHT SHE FELT the soft pull of rising road. They were passing between the medicine hills. Far away, through the crisp dark, she could see the fragile lights of town.

Home, people, all that had been reality, seemed like the dream now: foreign, impossible to go back into. If she kept on down the road and never stopped, could she put off going back, forever?

At the crossroads she turned toward the Haneys'.

She pulled into the yard and waited. Like her, they would look from the dark before exposing themselves to the disadvantage of a lamp. The horse blew and talked in whuffles, knowing where he was. Someone stood in the door. Then a lantern came and was raised to light her.

Mr. Haney, half-white nightshirt, half-black pants, put his bare foot on a spoke and lifted himself to bend close over the wagon bed.

"Name of God," he whispered.

The woman came in silence to the end of the wagon

and looked in. She reached her hand around Tater's ankle. Warm. Her face crumpled.

She took the lantern from Mr. Haney's fist. He dropped the saddle out on the ground and pulled the bedroll to the end of the wagon. He lifted Tater over his shoulder. A long skein of sound trailed after them as they went into the house.

The woman stood bulging in her white nightgown. She put her hand on Papa's leg, and drew it back in resignation.

She was shaped like a D, cresting. Going to full moon. Growing time. Madness. She looked at Lena and let the lantern down to the ground. When she untied the horse and stepped back, Lena drove away.

Claudie sat at the table. The Bible was open under the lamp. Lena stopped the wagon in the bar of light that fell from the window into the yard.

Claudie flung the door open. "Ben?"

I was spared this, Lena thought. I got to hear your voice, Papa. Thank you. "No," she answered, "me."

Claudie moved toward her, dressed, her hair flaring in the light. "Lena? Ben?" She felt along the wagon to the end. Lena got down and brought the lamp from the kitchen. From the porch she heard the scream, and saw Claudie bent over her hands, taking a blow she would never recover from.

Lena tried to touch her arm. Claudie screamed again and again and almost fell. Lena set the lamp at the end of the wagon and went in to keep the little ones from running out if they had heard.

She leaned in at the door of the lean-to. Innocent breath. Lord, rest them to be ready. She shut the door softly and went back outside.

Claudie sat beside Papa. Her screams had sunk to quivers of sound that shook her body. She held his unreal hand.

"Claudie, I'm sorry," Lena whispered. There was no answer but the shivers of desolation. She went in and got a blanket and laid it over Claudie's head and shoulders. She stood until she was needed.

"Tell me how did it happen," Claudie finally said.

"I just found him." She didn't know until she said it that it would come out that way. "At Hawk Hill."

"But somebody did this and they going to suffer for it if it takes the rest of my life."

Lena bit her lips and stood silent.

"Who? You have to tell me, Lena." In the blanket, she looked like every woman who had ever mourned.

"I can't remember."

"You can't remember?" Claudie rose tall upon her knees, staring her down. "You the best memorizer at school, and can say the Bible nearly through—and you can't *remember?*"

Lena gripped the sideboard of the wagon until Claudie sank down again. Didn't she know she couldn't seek revenge for Papa, of all people.

"Lena, we're not South now. We don't have to hold still for this anymore. We don't have to be scared to go to the law."

"I'm not scared." They had become strangers to each other. She did have to hold still, and let the first law work. Not because of other people's rules. Because she chose to.

"I can guess who," Claudie said.

"But you don't know. You won't ever."

"Lena! Can you let the person go free that did this?"

"I have to let God handle it, that's all." She broke suddenly into wild tears. "Papa didn't talk about any of that. He talked about loving us. He said we couldn't give up on—that person. And I didn't. And I won't."

Her mouth went to jelly. Her knee joints melted away. She clawed at the splinters. How was Tater ever going to heal, jittering along in a wagon, with no home?

Minutes moved past them. Slowly Claudie reached out over the side of the wagon and drew her close. "Oh, little girl," she whispered. "Big little girl, now. You going to be just like him. Lord have mercy." She lifted Lena's face and kissed it with quiet acceptance.

The lamplight spangled and blurred. The team sighed. Faithful . . . unharness . . . rest and water. Lena let go of the wagon, floated toward them, and fell to the ground.

At dawn she woke for a moment in her own bed, and saw Claudie sitting in the wagon, bent in her blanket, saying her last things. The team was gone. The lamp had burned out at Papa's feet.

Next a clatter jerked her out of sleep. Voices. She rose up shakily. Mrs. Chism and Jaybird Kelsey were getting out of Mrs. Chism's car. They must have promised Claudie the night before that they would begin a search as soon as it was light. Claudie walked toward them from the porch. She had put on her best dress and wound her head in a white cloth, and she would never look the way she used to look.

They stopped at the wagon. She heard Mrs. Chism's oath, and their silence. She lay back. Now it belonged to the town. They would fetch the preacher. Mr. Starnes would come. The sheriff, even. But not likely. Say I can't remember. Mrs. Chism tended to the legal business of her hired hands. Knew how. Flourished on contention, Papa had said.

Claudie came into the lean-to. Her eyes had sunk to rest in the swollen pillow of her face.

"Are you all right?" Lena asked.

"Yes." Claudie looked at the sleeping children. "Before Mr. Starnes comes with his hearse wagon. Do you want to—" Her mouth worked. "Say good-bye?" She was handing what had been hers over to the town now, and it was hard.

"I already did," Lena said softly.

"Then sleep," Claudie said. She looked down at Roy and Armilla under the quilt, making two hills planted with patchwork fields. "As long as you can."

She went out and shut the door.

The sun had passed across the window when Lena woke again. Two deep voices murmured in the kitchen. Roy and Armilla were gone.

She stumbled up, surprised she was still dressed, and found her shoes. When she opened the door, the preacher and Mr. Kelsey stood up from the table. Brother was playing with pan lids behind a barricade of chairs. Some of Mrs. Chism's leftover dinner sat in covered dishes. She had found guests for it after all.

Jaybird Kelsey said, "Miss Lena—" He suddenly put his hand on her shoulder, and as suddenly took it away.

The preacher cleared his throat and looked anxious. Mrs. Chism had rousted him out before he could shave. He murmured, "What can I say to you, Lena? You know all the words already."

Who comforted preachers? she wondered.

"Yessir," she said.

The black kitten walked out from behind Mrs. Chism's soup tureen. "Oh!" Mr. Kelsey said, embarrassed because he had been playing with it on the table. He scooped it up. It attached itself to his vest with tiny rose-thorn claws. Lena and the preacher each took up a paw while Mr. Kelsey unhooked the last two and set little Old Nick on the floor.

The other three crawled out from under the linen cup towel Mrs. Chism had brought something in. Lena's throat filled. While she had been gone they had opened their blue, blue eyes.

She put them out on the porch. The wagon was gone. The barn door opened, and Roy and Armilla came out, holding the hands of Winslow Starnes. They went around the corner toward the chicken yard. She could tell by the way they walked that they didn't know yet. She turned to Mr. Kelsey. "What's he doing here?"

"Mary, Tom, and I brought him out. He flagged us down when we passed him on the way to school. He had heard from his father what happened, and he wanted to come."

She stared out at him. "Does his father know he's here?"

Mr. Kelsey looked down the road where a wisp of dust was drifting. "Not yet. But he will in a minute."

Mr. Starnes got out of the black-curtained wagon and walked stiffly toward the garden where Claudie and Mrs. Chism stood. He was carrying a kind of long pole. He lifted his hat briefly to Mrs. Chism. They spoke past Claudie, then all three came slowly up the porch steps and into the house.

With a start Lena saw that the pole was a rolled-up stretcher. Jaybird Kelsey walked behind Mr. Starnes into the closed bedroom. A soft horror strangled her. She broke past them all and leaped off the porch. Papa had been in there since the first time Mrs. Chism and Mr. Kelsey came. They had put Sunday clothes over his wound, and folded his hands that had held on so hard. She knew these were the rites, the wall people put around their emptiness to give it shape, and she could let them do it. But they couldn't make her look. Because it had nothing to do with Papa, traveling far beyond their bounds.

She went behind the house and watched Roy and Armilla showing Winslow how to fill the chickens' water pan. Before he could get it filled, a hen hopped on its rim and flipped it over. Water gushed out over his shoes. The little ones squealed and helped him bring more.

She went back along the side of the house and looked around the corner. They were standing by the porch again. The covers of the wagon were fastened down. Claudie held the baby on her hip.

Mrs. Chism said, "You people always have a brother or a cousin or a uncle. Don't you have anybody back there that could make me a good hand?"

"Sisters, is all," Claudie said.

"I don't mean there can be as good a hand as Ben, damn it," Mrs. Chism said. Her mean old face turned away and she gazed into distance. "Well, maybe I can squeeze enough work out of those Haneys to get the crop in, and find me a new hand by spring. Maybe that Mexican jumping bean—" She turned to Mr. Kelsey. "Pablo? Pancho?"

"Pedro Garcia," Mr. Kelsey said. "I'll ask around."

Faquita's father. Lena crept around the corner.

Claudie said, "I thought the Haneys were moving."

"Moving? I was throwing them off. But damn it, I need somebody. They might as well stay now till that last baby's whelped and ready to travel."

A weight moved off Lena's heart. If they stayed till

132

spring, then Tater would have time to heal. She went suddenly to stand by Claudie.

"Well," Mrs. Chism said, fixing her on a fork. "I hear you don't know anything that happened." She studied Lena like a bite of something that might be spoiled. "Don't you know I can't help you if you won't speak up? You people make me so tired." For a second her eyes wavered. "But then I probably couldn't help anyway. That shoddy old coot I had the boundary dispute with—if he sent somebody over to scare off my man, he's already made plenty sure I can't prove it."

"Yes," Lena said. "Ma'am."

"So what are you going to do?" Mrs. Chism said to Claudie. She pulled Mr. Kelsey's watch out by the fob and looked at the time. All of them waited, speechless. "You know you're paid up to the first of the year. After that . . ."

Tears came into Claudie's eyes. She rubbed Brother's hair, blinking and swallowing to keep from breaking down in front of them all. Lena's throat got tight. She touched Claudie's arm.

"Claudie, we'll go back to Scattercreek if you want to. I'll go." It was all she had left to give her.

Claudie's soft mouth slowly made a line that Lena had never seen before. Her chin lifted. "This town is where your daddy brought you to have your chance. And this is where we stay. *Here*." She turned on Mrs. Chism. "I can wash and iron and work at any job. And so can Lena. We know how to earn our keep. And we know how to knuckle to you." Mrs. Chism's eyebrows shot up, but Claudie was looking past her, past them all. The tears she had forced back glinted like steel. "Only we mean to work and to knuckle the way we choose to, and where we choose to. I have two boys coming up to be the same threat to all you that Ben was. You better be ready for them, because I'm going to have them ready for you."

She stumbled up the porch steps and slammed the door. "Amen," the preacher said under his breath.

Mr. Starnes looked around and saw Winslow and the

little kids crawling through the pasture fence. His mouth dropped open.

"Boy, get yourself over here this minute," he yelled.

Winslow came forward with the little kids and stopped halfway across the yard.

"What the deuce are you doing here?" his father exclaimed. "You get yourself back to school before I take my belt to you."

Winslow looked at Lena. The color had gone out of his face, but his jaw jutted with determination. He cleared his throat. "I'm going to stay here, in case there's anything else I can do." He looked down at the little kids squeezed small along his legs. "Right now we're going for a walk. We have things to talk about."

He turned and started them back toward the fence.

"Now look here—" Mr. Starnes shouted after him.

Jaybird Kelsey took Mr. Starnes by the coat sleeve. "I'll stop by and tell the teacher. Let him be." He gazed after Winslow with a small, proud smile.

Mr. Starnes whirled on his heel, hunting something to aim his anger at. To nobody exactly he yelled, "One broken-down plow to pay for this? I'll go bankrupt, dealing with these people."

Mrs. Chism said, "Ben kept a good plow—worth two of your funerals, and you know it. Hell, it covers everything, Starnes. Everything. Everything."

She strode to her car. Mr. Kelsey hurried to open her door but was too late. He launched himself around to turn the crank. Lulu sat up in the seat. "Get out of the way, damn it," Mrs. Chism ordered. She squeezed herself in. The engine started.

The preacher watched anxiously to see if she was too angry to wait for him. "Tomorrow, then, Lena. The service will be at the cemetery, at eleven. I pray—" He looked at the door Claudie had slammed behind her. "I pray—" he began again, and turned and got into the car.

Mrs. Chism went roaring down the wagon track, scything weeds right and left. Mr. Starnes got up onto his wagon seat and followed with all the professional dignity he had left.

The kittens toppled out from under the porch, three little gray sisters and the strong one, their brother, bristling with life. The little pink pearls of their toe pads had already turned the color of the ground.

Lena walked to the fence where Winslow and the little kids had crossed into the pasture. The kittens straggled after her. Winslow looked taller than she remembered, walking slowly toward the river.

What will come to fill the empty space, Papa? The way the kittens came for Bullet. The way Claudie and your children came for you.

She stood listening, but not for the answer. Like him, it was already all around her and in her, promising wonders and mysteries, pounding with life.

What she heard was the faraway sound of the train starting out of town. The engineer had answered the conductor's highball wave with two sharp whistle blasts. She could feel the engine coming, growing, driving hard in ragtime. Two longs, a short, a wailing long. It had passed the first crossing and was curving toward the trestle, headed west.

Over on the far edge of their field, she saw a speck. It moved, and she thought she could see a dark humped back, a black hat. It looked like Mr. Haney out there, picking the last of their cotton for them.

She batted her eyes to be sure. He was the last person she expected to see. Claudie would say he thought he had to bargain with them not to tell what happened. Maybe that was why he was there. But maybe not. She shook her head slowly, the way Papa did when he meant wonders never ceased, and watched Mr. Haney pick their cotton, bent against the weight of his sack.

ABOUT THE AUTHOR

OUIDA SEBESTYEN had aspired to a career in writing since she was six years old. But, unable to spend the necessary amount of time required to learn her art, she wrote in "terribly earnest spurts which resulted in discouraging rejections. Four unsold adult novels and 50 unsold adult stories later, I decided I was writing for the wrong-sized people. When *Words by Heart* came pouring out, I felt I had found my niche." *Words by Heart* grew out of the author's familiarity with the West and her own family's struggle against hardship. While the work is fiction, Ms. Sebestyen adds that she drew upon stories of her parents and grandparents for a feel of the time. "Their struggles in a tiny Texas community helped shape the book. My aunt joined in supporting the family at 13, and saw all seven children through college. She, more than anyone, suggested the heroine." Quite coincidentally, that heroine was born in the same year as Ouida Sebestyen's mother. "After that, when I was uncertain about school lunches or girls wearing black stockings back in 1910, I just yelled into the kitchen and she'd yell back answers. I discovered that each question triggered enough of my mother's memories for another book." Ouida Sebestyen lives with her teenage son and her 80-year-old mother in Boulder, Colorado.